NOT GHOSTS, BUT SPIRITS

VOLUME V

Querencia Press – Chicago Illinois

QUERENCIA PRESS

© Copyright 2025
Querencia Press

ISBN 978 1 963943 35 1

www.querenciapress.com

First Published in 2025

Querencia Press, LLC
Chicago IL

Printed & Bound in the United States of America

CONTENTS

For When I Die

Don't forget to feed the cats;
There's a spare key to all my locked
Closets above the bathroom doorframe.

    Remember
    my name
    even when you can't
    remember
    my laugh

Grab the "just in case" pack of cigarettes
From my glove compartment before
My dad thinks I picked back up the habit;
There's a week's worth of food in the freezer to get you started;
Your taxes are in the right-hand drawer of my desk

    Remember
    my patience
    even when you can't
    remember
    my words

Don't neglect cleaning the toothpaste streaks
And mildew in the bathroom;
Flip the couch cushions regularly
And take the blankets to the dry cleaners

This should be a love letter
But instead it's become a list of chores;
Please take inventory of things
I embodied or inspired besides
Housework and taking care of others

Please don't let them bury me;
I'd rather collect dust on ~~our~~ your mantle.

—**Maggie Bowyer** (they/he)

Ode in cold season

Ode to easing the sick child back into a nap
to hearing each breath and the next, the subtle rise of her chest
to her eyelids heavy as the sea and just as still

Ode to the sun-filled window and an empty hour, more or less
to jasmine tea steaming on the sill
to looking out at copper leaves steadfast on oak branches

    and the soft cedars

    that surround them

    in everlasting green

Ode to linen and its nubby imperfections
to a hobby that warms the lap
to blue thread and a sharp needle
to lavender everything, lavender linen and lavender candles

    and last lavender light in winter's sunsets before the canopy goes navy

    when the blood moon burns through the trees

    and the guinea fowl   pepper   the silence

    with their anxious cries that are not

    unfamiliar at all to my soul

Ode to colors to coughs   to cries that jar me back into my body

    when all week I have hovered above it

    wondering what was the point of everything

    and how did we—all of us—get here and why why why

—**Sara Triana** (she/her)

Heaven Turned Moldy

From the day you are born you taste it.
It dances on the tip of your tongue.
A moment ago, I attempted suicide.
A moment ago, Dad sang and rocked me.

Call it hell or forgotten memory.
Every person you used to be—every person
Buried. Who hasn't tasted flames? They
Lick you up like little things come easy.

—Poverty, loneliness, vacancy.
Nighttime faraway inside me.
Daddy is singing nursery rhymes.
Tone deaf and smiley, he's rocking me.

Forever that didn't have time to stay.
Heaven turned moldy. Breath,
Like hell, is catching. Little things
Come easy—hell comes easy.

Try and remember heaven. The singing;
The cradling. The way when I was a baby,
Something humble happened to me.
Warmth and kindness there.

If only I could remember. But
Breath, like heaven, is quick to leave.
Breath, like heaven, is a pilgrim.
I only taste forgetting. When Dad

Was young, he can't remember me.
Fatherhood somewhere inside him.
I bet it felt like fire. I bet it licked him up
Like little things are heartbreaking.

Dad is cradling the body of a baby.
I'm told the child is still inside me.
Daddy rocks me close to his chest,
He holds a wooden picture book.

That was a spark, now I turn red.
Not singing. Not rocking.
Burning. Burning.
I am forgetting my future.

Thoughts of suicide cradle me.
I swallowed the child inside me.
I pray she is somewhere safe.
(I fear she is also burning.)

I didn't know his voice would make
Me hungry. Hunger, fire, breathe.
"Not yet", "until", "for now".
I'm sure you know what I mean.

If not, continue eating. Keep on,
Keep on returning. It's all in
Your head, your body. Heritage is
Always happening. Heaven,
Like a pilgrim, was only visiting.
Daddy who holds me is gone.
Breath, like hell, is catching.
Thoughts of suicide rock me.

—Maya Collins (she/her)

First published by Anti-Heroin Chic

**to the adult who loves crows too much and commiserates
about the world ending just enough**

how can you love crows so much
and still misnomer them as blackbirds?
I get it, I also grew up without crows

my only reference point, looking and pointing
a blackbird! becoming a crow was painful and obvious
to practice flying: impossible in these conditions.

yet she flies. do not mistake her for a blackbird.

—Wilfred Jensen (they/them)

Adaptive Behavior II – Kathy Bruce (she/her)

X

when I first came out I had all these timelines I wanted to meet
I was thinking *how can I manifest destiny?*

and everyone's got this idea that it's all about *attainable goals*—
you set long & short term things to achieve &

you write the pathway to realization & you go through
with it & most importantly   you believe

if I think about it hard enough, will my tits just disappear?
one of my short term goals was getting a new license

because the state of New York had just said
anyone can have any letter they want and we're even doing X!

I was really thrilled about that, so I filled out the paperwork
and marched all the way across the island &

I posed for a sweaty photo—hair thick with gel &
barely a hint of a smile because *that's* masculinity—

& I handed everything to the person behind the counter &
they rang me up & gave me the temporary license to give a once-over—

thanks!—and *god dammit!*   there it was clear as day just like the chat goes off
when someone dies in a video game: *F*

& it took all of my bloody energy to say *um actually*
I do not want it this way!

& we went through the whole rigmarole again & finally
a month later I got my shiny new license in the mail with the tiny x—

and it was so much smaller than I thought it would be
& like   I wasn't even excited anymore

—**Alexandra Servey** (they/them)

The Author Martyrs Himself in This One

Unflinching yet changing,
the way snow melts & ruins all your shoes.

Salt-tongues & empty promises
it's the mental illness, remember?

You've gotta love the ones who fuck up the most
just like in the bible or whatever.

I'm trying to figure out a way to feel bad about
the things I did when I was unmedicated.

I sang promises like a bird during the mania
& the partying which always makes the

comedown worse. I become a box of matches in
love with a house fire. It's like I am ash and smoke.

Do you get what I'm saying? It's *"I'm sorry"* in a
million different languages except the ones I'm fluent in.

Desculpe.   Lo lamento.   Paenitet. Gomen'nasai.

I am taking one for the team.

—**Gabriel Noel** (he/him)

First published by new words {press}

Noctalgia

I have given
all the words I have
for him. A jawless skull.
They tumbled loose
into the dirt

& we stare
at them like seeds
in need of burial,
can't leave them
naked on the earth,
spilled,

nor bring ourselves
to plant them.
Years later,
someone asks how
we met & we kiss

like rain,
in case the world is
ending & streetlights
burn the cataract
of milky way
from night.

—**Jason Clemmons** (he/him)

A Letter to My Uterus

Hi there. It's me.

I know we don't talk much, but I've been thinking about you lately.

Maybe you already know this. Like how the brain communicates movement through the spinal cord to the feet. Can you sense the tapping of my thoughts along your wall? Maybe you're talking to me too.

I'm writing because I have a lot of questions. Admittedly, more than I probably should as a woman approaching 30. But there is still a lot I don't understand about you. For starters, I'm hoping you can tell me, *what is it that you do, exactly?*

Okay, sure. I'm not entirely clueless. I learned about you in health class, but that was more than a decade ago, and let's face it, the quality of sex education delivered by my high school health teacher who was also my field hockey coach is, well, debatable.

When I turned 16, my mom took me to see a gynecologist. Her gynecologist, to be exact—also known as the man who delivered me from her. I guess you could say our relationship had come full circle. A diagram of you hung on the wall of the exam room. I should have studied it but I kept my gaze fixed on the ceiling. The doctor and nurses never referenced it either. Perhaps they saw your luscious pink lining more as a decoration, a fine way to cover white space.

I could go on but I think you see where I'm coming from by now. I am a full-grown woman who can vote, buy a car, own a home, file taxes, and yet, I *still* don't understand how my body works. The older I get, the more I realize just how little I know about you. Yet, I have never *not* known you. It's a bit ironic, don't you think? Funny even. That is until it's not. There are many things it scares me not to know but I fear the answers too.

Sometimes I type your name into Google. *Hollow. Muscular. Pear-shaped.* This is how the Internet describes you. But to me, you look more triangular. Your outer lining, a shield. The Cleveland Clinic says you're small enough to fit in my hand, which surprises me. I imagined you larger. But you can grow, can't you? How big? I read somewhere that you can regenerate too. That you're one of only two organs with this power. Tell me, is this true?

I'll admit you and I haven't always been on the best of terms. Your heavy crimson flow and aching cramps taunted me for days back when I slid tampons up my sleeves on the way to Algebra. I worried even the thickest of pads wouldn't be enough to contain the overflow of boiling stew in between my legs. My period hardly ever arrived on the day circled in my calendar and I resented you for it. Like when I found your bright red spots in my underwear the day of Sara's pool party. Or when you stained my favorite pair of shorts with a brownish hue that never did quite come out.

Then, at 17, there was the first ovarian cyst. Doubled over on the bathroom floor. A stinging, no—stabbing pain. Like a jagged knife penetrating the flesh. In the emergency room—after six hours of blood tests, urine samples, x-rays, an ultrasound—the nurses *finally* figured out what was wrong. The doctor suggested I go on birth control to prevent future cysts. The only reason my mom agreed was because it was for "medical reasons." We ignored the possibility of any others. That was more than ten years ago. I've taken the pill every day since.

For a long time, this seemed like a smart decision. The obvious choice even. Every girl I knew in college was on some form of birth control, but I don't remember any of us questioning what it was doing to our bodies. Did you wonder where the cramping and spotting and mood swings all went? Do you remember how it felt when your lining grew thicker? Do you miss having a "real" period? *I don't.* The fatigue. The hunger. The hormones. They're all symptoms, I'm learning, of how my body caters to you. Of the sacrifices it makes in pursuit of delivering you a seed fertile enough to grow. All the while, here I am, fighting against the very thing science says you're designed to do.

Now I hear horror stories from women whose bodies transformed into foreign terrain after they went off the pill. I worry the same could happen to me. Besides, we're gay now. If it weren't for the cysts, we wouldn't even need birth control. Sometimes I think about all the anxiety and money I could have saved on $20 pregnancy tests if I had figured out my sexuality sooner. Tell me, did you know? Was it you I felt tightening in my gut the nights I spent in the beds of boys who left me hollow and dry? I'm sorry you had to experience such an invasion. I wish I could have protected us better, saved us from the pain I inflicted while trying to convince myself the pain felt good.

The question of whether I want children or not is one I'm still debating. Actually, that's not true. I've thought about this a lot and for as long as I can remember there has been something inside me saying motherhood is not for me. I can't quite place where it comes from, but I'm curious if you sense it too. Even still, I find myself questioning what it would mean to carry a child.

They say the brain can numb memories of childbirth. This way, we're more likely to do it again. Some may call this evolution but to me, it sounds a lot more like deception. I imagine long stretch marks over a protruding belly. Swollen feet at the end of the day. Backaches. Tender breasts. Diarrhea. Nausea. But I can't see any of this actually happening to me. I'm still in disbelief that my body could shapeshift in such ways. That you—everything—could change.

I think I'd like to freeze my eggs just so I could look at them. Study them in all their elusiveness. Hold in my hands, a wonder of my body, my womanhood. If I could see them, maybe they would feel more real. Maybe so would you. At last, there would be evidence of my inherently female anatomy I have sometimes doubted exists at all.

This dissonance, I suspect, is the source of my apathy toward motherhood. But why must there be something to blame? Why do I continue to subscribe to the narrative that motherhood is something I *should* want? But tell me, do you think it's selfish of me to deny you? Am I robbing you of your potential? Are you longing to be full, to fulfill your *natural* purpose?

I read about a study the other day where researchers tested how the brain and uterus communicate by experimenting on rats. They removed the uterus from one group, the ovaries from another, and in some rats, both. Then they tested each rat's ability to navigate a maze, modifying the route over time to assess how the rats responded. Now that I'm writing this, I'm thinking about how unfair this experiment was to the rats, but it did produce some interesting findings. The rats without a uterus had a harder time navigating the maze. They suffered from spatial memory loss, or to put it simply, they struggled to find their way.

I'll admit, at times when I have felt exhausted by how your needs often trump mine, I've pondered what it would mean to free my body of you. In ancient Greece, the cause of hysteria, a misdiagnosis assigned *only* to women, was thought to be a roaming uterus. The solution was to take the uterus out, a hysterectomy, as it's still called in medicine today. Placing the blatant sexism of this aside, I wonder if maybe the Greeks were onto something. I never considered what parts of myself may be lost in your absence. What pocket of emptiness may exist when you're gone. Without you, I wonder if I too would lose my way.

I know you mustn't like going to the doctor's office. I don't either but I've been trying to figure out why a flash of pain, you know the one, still comes sometimes in the same spot as that first cyst. It only lasts a few seconds when I move or stand too quickly, but it's enough to freeze me into a forward bend until it subsides.

In the exam room, I lay on my back, eyes up at the ceiling, while my doctor squeezes ice blue lubricant onto the tip of a 12-inch wand before sliding it inside me. They say it's not supposed to hurt. They being the doctors and ultrasound technicians and WebMD but it does. Every muscle inside me flinches and I try to relax when she tells me to but I can't and I'm sure you can't either.

We're getting close to having done this nearly a dozen times and I'd like to stop but the cysts keep coming back and we still don't know why. This doctor is good though. Better than the ones who pressed and probed as if the half of my body above my waist wasn't there. I can see everything on the ultrasound TV next to me and she explains each step, reassuring me along the way.

In the last exam, as she moved the wand from my right side to my left, a shushing sound echoed from the machine.

Swoosh. Swoosh. Swoosh.

"That's the blood flowing to your uterus," she said.

I titled my head closer, surprised by how strong you sounded. Surprised to hear a sound coming from you at all. Why had I never heard you like this before?

For a moment, I forgot about the discomfort between my legs. I pictured your walls vibrating, your lining swelling in size. A current of blood making your hollowness whole, filling you, me, with strength. A rhythmic power. Like ocean waves crashing on the shore.

I wonder if you'll always sound this way. Or if you may quiet as we age. Will I still be able to hear you in another decade from now? What about two?

I imagine you must know what's coming. That you were born with the knowledge of how things will end. Me, I'm not certain of what the future for us holds. But I'll be here, listening for you. Even if your rumbling softens to a whisper.

Sincerely, yours.

—**Kate Warrington** (she/her)

What's held hostage, hm?

What's held hostage, hm?   in the folds of her belly
those lost chins and Spanx up the wazoo—literally up there
burning out the ingrown hairs with stains of exhaustion
but she can outdance them—feels a trickle of satisfaction
as those youth peel from their stagnant dancefloor shuffles
leaving this helicopter-stomping tornado as a singular bonfire
ebullition of abandon washing forth with ovarian violence
nothing matters more than the beat, in the folds of her belly

—**Zephyris** (they/them)

Grief is a Plant – Kathleen Baker (she/her)

excommunicated

our connections are fraying—
knots held together by single threads
left out to weather for 15 years
of unwanted-unneeded-unnecessary
of me
the extraneous wild child
whose will could not be broken
by bible by guilt by paddle

go ahead and try to
convince me that i've
always
really
mattered
when we are equidistant
but somehow your 500 miles
are so much farther than mine
and my 500 miles
have never been fucking far enough
when your faith in god
meant more than my life
and my faith in god
burned up behind the wheel
when i left you in the rearview mirror

you can't tell me now
this wasn't your own fault
selfishly wielding your scissors
for the past 35 years
c o n t i n u a l l y
cutting back who i am
into who i was
who i became
into who i should have been
until there are only memories
of a girl in a floral dress who is
baptized-saved-redeemed
singing hymns and
whispering prayers and
hiding from your expectations

—until—

somewhere along the line
i found my own scissors
and carved myself a home
in this body this brain this being
until i stand unrecognizable
as the daughter i once was
done waiting for your sorrys
done asking for your forgiveness—
not yours not His not anyone's
servant anymore

so close your mouth now
please—
there are no excuses left

—**Chriss Locker** (they/them)

I want to build a house with you more often than I want to die

I want to build a house with you more often than I want to die:
cooking stove, red pot, pine tree. I want to assemble a bookcase,
I want—my books & your books, all in the same place. I want
the grey in your hair, the one you hate so much. The laugh lines
you so deeply dread. I want a dog, & a cat, & your horses.
Cottage by the edge of town, like in that silly movie
we watched for Christmas. Let's imagine it still snows,
somehow. Let's keep dreaming for a few months.
Starting off years with twelve kisses & counting roses
for Valentine's Day. One for each time you've made
my heart somersault. Room flooded, & you in the middle.
& because I want so much—endless mornings,
fresh flowers, drunk walk home—& because, for some
unknown miracle, you want so too, I leave the pills in their bottle.
I empty the bathtub, I put down the knife, I make my bed &
wait for you to call me back. I decide I don't want to go without
the mariachi band, without the twinning I do, without your hand in
my hand. Because I sleep with your t-shirt under my head, even
when we fight. Because you love the worst versions of myself.
Because when I do leave, I want to be certain I'll find you
again & again, patiently waiting,
a breeze through the trees, sunlight on my fingers,
grass under my skin.

—**Dante Émile** (he/they)

SAD (Seasonal Affect Disorder)

the calendar's voice is dark / even brine salt is gray / an endless hourglass / gray goes
black / it still surprises me / sneaks up on me / *Time to turn the clocks back!* /
restlessness creeps in on a drunken moon / my vinyl blinds won't lie flat / the grimy
strings, a midnight noose / who makes up names for all the babies anyway?

i trip on an extension cord / sink into every stain / a million exclamation points pierce my
skin / feelings bleed out / my pills run out / i string despondent bras over a mirror / crawl
into an empty space / swallow an invisible blanket / wait for mermaids to sing

i'm not thinking a damn thing / but go mad when my rind splits open / ornaments of a
broken
life / i count backwards / wait for the moon to sober up / even the clock won't talk to me
/ can a lizard grow back from a single cell?

i remember floating on the beach under rays of light / a lover's hand in my pocket, melting
        loneliness / when i looked good photographed naked / when i remembered my name
/ the sun must be a lonely star

i'm out of wine again   retreat   resign   resolve   escape in my nightie to kiss the
        cold sidewalk   open my mouth like a goldfish waiting to be found.

—**Sherry Shahan** (she/her)

something like virginia

i burned the spider's web
with the match for my candle
soft smoke rising
as i turned back to my other tasks
small pieces of survival
accounts and numbers, hair on the carpet, coins for the laundry

later
lying on the couch
weary from a day i can't remember
saw her silhouette moving
to rebuild in the middle of the night
glow from our apartment courtyard
backlit her delicacy
her tenderness
her spiny limbs and
crushable bulb heart
i so admired her strength

i need to clean the pot of soup we had for dinner, the dishes in the sink, the boy needs lunch
tomorrow, there are words waiting for reply always hovering just above

feeling the need to dust
wipe her life into my cloth again
instead,
i welcome her home
let myself rest
watch her great and gentle work

—**Ashley Howell Bunn** (she/they)

Shower Conversation

If there's nothing
at the end of the tunnel,
then I have eaten dirt
for nothing.

I speak to echoes
in drains.
They tell me that I am, and

and nothing can
nothing can be if I
do not love myself

myself
and them.

They are myself,
I think,
they say.

I say,
"But I have no way to know."

They say,
"No."

—**Hannah Rowell** (she/her)

Permanent Pothole

Close your eyes. And try again. Alas,
      I gaze into the looking glass.

     No, Alice
There is no wonderland in the body,
I stare back at my stretched skin, now foggy.
I had become a universal mold & still, I left
this sag of my corpse, not dead just famished.
I've hidden the world's lesions in glitter, damn it!

Alice, did you know that being a girl
is being a pothole in a city
demanding your refill?

     No, Alice,
The Cheshire Cat is not real,
Please. I am tired of the squeal—
the squeeze of throat
as snug as my mother's lost coat.
But if he's real, teach me his craft of distortion.
Allow my escape! Pressed against the screen—
even nature is vengeful—
the windowed flashes reveal my contortion
& I hear Gaia cradle me blind
& I'm almost relieved.

Alice, why did no one tell us that sight—
this want—would blight?

I think about if the glass wanted to be looked at
I think about the tragedy in reflection.
Unable to produce no more beyond
the subject. How in all its retellings, never considered.
Alice, are we afterthoughts, or is that too much?

     No. Alice.
I am not a girl with ghosts in her closet.
     Alas, Alice.
Wonderland is not the rabbit hole.
Wonderland is the right gender.

Wonderland is like God, unattainable.

Alice.
Hear the storm envy how loud I thunder—
agonize a crawl toward respect &
cling to glass ceilings we called mirrors &
gawk at my bulge as its shadow murders me.

I stand before that hole
in the ground, my hole.
This city's pothole. Being a girl
with a dick in this city means I
am the worst pothole. I
am a permanent pothole. Unfillable
& I never did feel full. My flesh protrudes
like the jagged shards glistening in my hand,
reflecting furrowed brows and hairy underneath.
Alice. This is the looking glass.

    Alas. Close your eyes. And try again.

—**Alé Cota** (they/she)

bitter pill

The shortcut through Montlake on the way to his house in Madrona winds its jagged path. It always takes precision, she thinks, threading through the neighborhood—like opening a combination lock. Tonight, she knows she is taking it too fast, and rather than brake to slow down, she shifts down from third into second. The engine revs, a roar like that of a wounded beast, then she's through. She sails the rest of the way. All the way to him. His house is white and tall, its golden light pouring through the windows. As usual, the door has been left open. As she climbs the stairs, she hears his guitar. A soulful tune she hasn't heard before. She likes it and tells him so when she comes in.

You do? He jokes, batting his eyes like a child greedy for a mother's love. He's being silly, but it's true. He wants her to say that she likes it again.

It's really good, she says and smiles.

Then they're on his bed, and she is looking at him in his wool sweater, ecru against his dark hair. She wants to do this thing with him, she thinks. *This is love.*

She needs to tell him but doesn't want to say *"pregnant."* It feels ugly in her mouth and makes her think of other words like it like *stagnant, repugnant, combatant.* But she can't say it any other way. She won't say she's *with child.* It's too archaic.

I have something to tell you, she says. *I'm pregnant.* The word will do its work.

His eyes widen, blue-bright against his dark eyelashes. His eyes streaked with white seem to churn like ocean waves. He wants to go back to the moment before. To the moment before she came, back to when she was on her way and the idea of her, this sexy woman coming over, driving across the city in her little yellow sports car and coming to him—to be with him, to have sex with him in his bed—intoxicated him so much that it fueled his creativity. He almost had something extraordinary. A new song. It was on the edge of his fingertips. There is no way to recall it now.

Her voice is soft. Almost a whisper. *It's a lot to take in. I know,* she says, *but tell me. I want to know how you feel.*

Well, to be honest, I'm upset, he says, his breath a gasp.

He wonders how this could have happened, but he knows how, and it might be his fault. They had wanted nothing between them, before they stopped and did the responsible thing, and he was the one who chose how long to go. But that doesn't mean he wants a child right now. He loves her. He doesn't need to look at her to remind himself. But they aren't ready yet. They need more time. This whole thing could so easily fall apart.

He hasn't spoken, and she wants him to say something, so she says, *I know it's not ideal timing.* She strokes his shoulder. Blinks. Watches. They're in his room on the third floor of the group house, the cedar tree beckons outside the window, the moisture of fall seeping in through the walls. There is mildew in his clothing because he keeps it in the attic off his room. It makes him smell older or old fashioned.

Yeah, he says, *I'm really not sure what we should do.*

He says this because he wants to say what sounds right, but he knows what they must do. They should put this baby off. He wants time for the music thing, but after that he sees a future for them. He thinks if they delay, their love could be a gleaming city. A lifelong marriage. A civilization. But if they have this baby now, it's a ramshackle world. A half existence.

I want us to make this decision together, she says.

She prides herself on being the kind of woman who responds to the needs of men. Who doesn't write them off in the name of feminism. But what she really wants is for him to agree with her.

The timing is terrible, he says. *I am really serious about us. I want us. Not anyone else.*

I know. It's early, she says. *This is all so new.*

It's true that they've only been together a few months. She knows how this thing isn't entirely perfect. Sometimes she gets mad at him and they fight.

But I think we can handle it, she says. *And I'll do most of the work.*

He looks at her, and his thick dark eyebrows make the crease.

I will, she insists.

She knows this is an absurd statement, but she feels it could be true, and wants it to be, that she could be a good mom, that she could give up her own selfishness in a way her mother did not.

He runs his fingers through his hair as he looks away. She is not thinking clearly, he thinks. He will have to be strong for both of them.

I don't want us to be a separated or divorced couple. I don't want to raise a kid that way. That is absolutely not what I want.

That's not what I want either.

He looks down at his fingers because they ache. New calluses from rehearsal last night. The new band is working. This is the first time he's been the leader, and not shared that role with anyone. He was leading, and leading well; they were deferring to him, matching him, and he was challenging them. The music was alive, flowing. Even the words were coming, as if from a new place in him.

Having a baby right now is not what I would choose.

She laughs. *I know, me either. I haven't chosen it either, but...*

His face flashes red; he's angry for such a split second that she's not sure what she's seen. He is thinking of his band and how they might really stand a chance. His mind screams, *Don't take this away from me! I'm only 26—I'm not ready!* but he doesn't say anything. He puts her hand in his and looks at her tenderly.

Just give me time to keep at this music thing, he says. *Please, I need time.*

Her eyes fill with tears, and her gut churns. *I hear you,* she says. *You need time.* She pats him on the back and looks out the window at the branches of the bending tree.

He says he's sorry but this is what he feels. *And I want us to be married first, and to have time to be married, time for the two of us to be alone. Perhaps three years, so that we can be solid before the children come.*

This is not exactly a proposal of marriage, but she sees his beautiful dream. The two of them happily married and having children, the picket fence of it all. It's something she barely believes in, but he seems to have the power to grant this. He seems more put together than she, more capable of enduring love, less chaotic, less wounded. His parents are still married. He has words that he strings together so easily, songs that flow through him. Maybe he can give her some of his certainty. Maybe he is right that their relationship wouldn't survive under the strain of a baby right now. So what if she's twenty-eight, and a baby is what her body wants. What her heart wants. Maybe she can wait.

She makes the appointment at a clinic called *Ariadne,* which makes her think of spiders and witches and the underworld. The sign has a woman in silhouette under the moon; the figure is of a young woman who makes her own choices; it is meant to make her feel empowered. But she isn't. They are at the clinic, sitting side by side, waiting. He plays the part of the gentle impregnator and kindly holds her hand. As she looks around the room and sees he is the only man there, she thinks maybe she should consider herself lucky just to have the kind of guy who would come with her.

A nurse brings ibuprofen and water in a small dixie cup and suggests she take it preemptively for pain. The cup shakes in her hands. If the water had been up to the edge, it would have spilled. But it doesn't. It ripples as if in response to an earthquake. Then with the pill in the one hand and the cup in the other, she turns to him and asks, "Should I take it?"

He doesn't understand the question when he says *Yes, of course. Take it.*

This is when she meets the decision, where she is forced to make it, because if she were to keep the baby, she wouldn't take this pill. If she were to keep the baby, she would protect it from the slightest bit of everything, even from this ibuprofen. This marks the end of the pregnancy, this moment in the waiting room, and not what happens hidden away even from her in the back room.

After, he walks her to her car. Her insides are scraped out and heavy. Blood is on her mind. She stands at her car in the dark. His is around the block. Their two homes are in opposite directions and far apart.

He says, *Are you sure you're okay?* and *Maybe I should drive you home. We could come get your car tomorrow.*

But things are different between them. This may be their new beginning, but she doesn't want to be with him tonight.

On the way home she thinks of calling her mother, and the conversation begins in her mind. Her mother would say *Hello* in her rich deep voice. Then hearing who it is, she would say *Darling!* and instantly her mother would know, just from the way her daughter says *Hi Mom, it's me* that something is terribly wrong. The explanation would come out in a flurry of tears, and immediately her mother would cry too. She hates when her mother cries about her problems, but that's not why she doesn't call. She doesn't call because if she is to have a future with this man, her mother can't know about the baby. Because if her mother knew what this man was asking, she would never forgive him.

Later, she's home. The woman she lives with is out, so she sits on the blue shag rug in the living room, Thai food boxes open and lined up in a row in front of her. The TV is so close that she can reach the knob, but it doesn't matter what she's watching. What matters is that she eats. First the fish cakes one by one, all of them, their crispy outsides and mushy insides, the orange, sticky, sweet sauce, the chunks of ridged raw cucumber. The noodles, wide and oily and seared on the edges. Down go chunks of deep-fried tofu, garlic, basil, red and green pepper. She is slender and her belly fills right away, but she keeps going. Too much food is not what she wants, but the fullness helps. She nearly fits it all inside. It's only when she can't eat another thing that she cries.

—**Lael Cassidy** (she/her)

The Author Offers Himself a Paradox

Let's say
when you were young
you never closed your heart off
like a wicker basket.
Say you
actually tell someone
that your body is written in
a language you don't understand
& you find yourself in a life
you thought you
lost.

Would you go looking for
all those forgotten fixed points?

Let's say
you wished you were lighter.
You swallow all the yellow
& try to match the sun
but no one cares to call
poison control.
Say you're
sick to death with missed chances,
your body hovers over barrels
waiting for vomit but
only spilling up time
instead.

Would you take back
what you said about god?

—**Gabriel Noel** (he/him)

NO! – Irina Tall (Novikova) (she/her)

The Nightjar Host

Among the husks of autumn
—studying for heaven
in a winter's den—
I am giving everything
I have to be here,
nesting
       with angels once broken
out west on fences, on beaches
where they fell to earth, or torn
from the wolf-jaw of America.

I draw each one a new
constellation
in the freckles of my chest,
promise in the spring
I'll map them
to the stars.
       This is a temporary place
to be abandoned; the lonely
nightjar keeps time, chanting
its name into darkness.

—Jason Clemmons (he/him)

In San Antonio (days after Uvalde)

We were shuffling with my mother and our kids along the crowded section of the riverwalk full of tourists who were sweating under umbrellas eating fajitas and swigging margaritas to-go when I thought what easy targets we all were. *My palm goes straight to my heart.* I heard a child wailing on the steps of a stone bridge over the opaque green water and it took me right inside that classroom, the forty minutes of terror, the golden hour they say police wasted as they debated how to enter, as they checked their phones, sanitized their hands. I try not to imagine the sounds but here by the bridge the children are in my ears. *I shake my head to clear their cries.* When we sat down for dinner somewhere they said the locals go, we ordered the kids a mountain of chips and toasted to surviving the summer heat with cold drinks as the host guided a family to the table next to ours. A father and boys and a little sister—she was laughing and you could tell they loved her for that. She always had a little *haha* in the corner of her gappy smile and they always had more jokes for her, more laughs, eyes leaking with delight. Every family *here* is forty miles from being a family *there.* I searched the dad, wondering how he doesn't grab them all in his arms and run, why I don't now before it happens again. Because it always happens again. The little sister waved at my daughters, sparkling with recognition, like *"we could be friends!" I gulp my drink to choke down my screams.* After we were home and the girls were in their beds, I sat on the front porch, watching the elevator glide up the Tower of the Americas, lights across the bottom, lights across the top. Up and down, it never stops.

—**Sara Triana** (she/her)

Gynandromorphism

a miracle is living two lifetimes in one body
defy biology, mimic nature.

no cycles only spirals. it mushes
on the inside before it morphs

or births. becoming a mother is death
cut into a chrysalis. see the same

cocoons and wombs carry tea parties
stay in there as long you need

9 months or 29 years
beautiful is to be indescribable

but try conceiving yourself while pregnant
take a Plan B prescribed by society

a frontal cortex stores more fear
with hormones. inject to restart

—**Hamsa Fae** (she/they)

Pleasure

                                       those fingers are yours
you could choose to touch, to pleat my skin   in feathers
in shudders   cavernous voids crashing in tumbling into the dark velvet womb
the heat swollen to decadence, and I would disappear
is that not the crux of pleasure—   to vanish
addicted to insensibility   the antidote to boredom

                                   your smile is yours to give
I crave it your impenetrable laugh   dreaming of kisses I will never receive
because   you say you would make a terrible lesbian
                  and

      we all stand guard for our psyches   monitor our sometimes variable selves
around dainty zodiacal lights   a balance scale with inborn calibration
time is ours to play out   in measured beats   the inconsistent tempo
always craving

                           dreams of undressed cheesecake
and cream-filled puff pastry   buttery flakes   falling into my cleavage as I bite
tickling and scratching at my underwire   laughing as I spill out the renegade crumbs
        and you   jokingly?   nuzzle in to lap them up

                                               —**Zephyris** (they/them)

Third Circle

Like a vein—
I mean it when I bleed.
A tender burn—a scream
caught in the chords. A low growl—Cerberus at the door.

I cannot stop the stampede of blood; hooves against the heat
of a compulsion—
a need to bury the greasy bone.

I mean it
when I wretch—
tongue rolling back and forth; a mouthful of earth.

I rise
and feast at the table of my Gorgon sisters.
We howl
a confession
that will never sanctify the original wound.

I rise to lick
the scars into submission. Like a vein—
I mean it when I bleed.

I sacrifice
a pound of flesh
to the dogs that would be kings.

—**Vignette-Noelle Lammott** (she/her)

The Magicians

We are what the magician made us. That is all. I cannot remember what we were before, but I think it was not this. We hop and flutter, eyes bright, heads cocked. We jump from branch to branch. We are not caged, not by bars, not with locks and keys, only clipped wings. We sing and chirp. The magician likes to hear our song.

I think we may have been girls once, playing in the glen. The sun caught in our hair, little voices lifted in laughter, we did not know the danger. I cannot now remember how it happened. A bird's memory is shorter than a girl's.

I remember this: his whisper in my ear, "Sing, my bright ones, for I have given you wings."

What are clipped wings but merely arms that flap uselessly against the sky?

We sing. We sing our mourning. We cry out for our lost voices, lost memories. The magician smiles. He does not understand the language of birds.

The magician thinks of many things. He does experiments in the night. For days he may not sleep or eat. He comes out every morning to walk among the trees where we roost so we may sing for him.

But the great magician is distracted, thinking of how to turn copper into gold. As we forget all trace of who we were, our flight feathers begin to grow back.

One morning he comes, and the light through the trembling leaves dapples his face green and sickly.

He says, "Sing," in his tired voice, and we do.

We sing as we peck out his eyes.

***

There is a magician in the forest who has no eyes. That is the legend they tell anyway. They say he steals away maidens. He turns them into birds, pretty trillers, cheap as trinkets.

They say it just to scare us, to keep little girls out of the forest, to keep us compliant, to keep us from the wild. Sometimes we go into the forest in search of him. We hide in the ferns, and the birds sing around us, and we do not really believe in the magician.

There is an old hermit who lives in the forest. He has no eyes. He mutters madness, and we bring him bread to eat.

He dries great fronds and flowers and herbs in his cottage and pounds them down to dust. He mixes in a little water, a little wine, and he makes a poultice for his dead eye sockets. He wraps white cloth around his head. He says it will let him see once more.

The birds chitter away like they are laughing at him.

"I used to be," he tells us sadly, "more than this." The poultice does not work. The poultice never works.

One day the hermit lies down in the garden, and he does not get up again. We mound rocks over him, and vines grow up between the stones, and the birds land among the leaves and sing and sing and sing.

And suddenly we can see everything. Back in the cottage we see the beakers, the salt, the pestle. The stinging nettles, the lightning moss. The copper and sage, the iron and ashblossom. We see the wine, the acid, and oil. There is wolfsbane, silverthorn, rowan berries. There are herbs and poisons, tinctures and opiates, potions and poultices. We see it all and we know what to do.

We turn the copper into gold. We are the magician now.

***

There are a pair of magicians; they live in the woods. We girls of the village go to their cottage twice a week bringing our foraging baskets. We wear flower crowns and the magicians teach us to weave spells with our hands, to turn metal into gold. We sing sweet songs with the birds to the bees and they sip nectar from the flowers that grow rampant, soaking up the sun.

The men in the village purse their lips with disapproval. They say the forest is dangerous, but we know it is not so. The magicians will always protect us. The magicians were girls just like us once. Then they drank the magic up like bees drinking nectar, and now they share all they've learned with us.

The village is small and dark and afraid. They do not like their girls full up on magic. The women do not say anything. They dare not contradict their husbands, but deep down we know they wish they were us.

In the night the men come. They drag us from our beds out to the square, and they light the pyre. Our feet scald and we cry out. The men's faces are set in stone, eyes glittering with flames from their torches. Their set mouths say, *this is what happens to girls who want too much.*

The heat closes in like arms, like heavy curtains, like licking mouths. The smoke obscures the stars.

Then there is a great cawing, screeching, flapping, and the birds of the woods are upon them, clawing and pecking. The birds call to us, and we raise our arms—which are suddenly wings—and we rise into the air, every girl of us, and we fly from the smoke into the forest in a great rustling flock.

We never go back to the village. We sing with the birds and the magicians, and we have never been happier.

—**Krista Beucler** (she/her)

Crowing

A little bit of girlhood, a little bit of cherry wine.
Crows begin to rest in the corners of our eyes.
Our laughs leave residue like stardust in the creases of
our cheeks. Silver strikes strands of hair like lightning in
a rain storm, leaving us forever changed. Age leaves its mark.
But we are fables. We are legends. We are in our girlhood,
forevermore in our little corner of the
cosmos.

—**Odette Augustine** (she/her)

Disengaged Desire – Kathy Bruce (she/her)

Scenes of Throwing Her Out and Finding Him

I'm in my closet sifting through all of my clothes attempting to figure out which fabrics, shapes, and sizes fit; trying to identify who I am through my clothing or something like that. I start a pile of skirts, dresses, frills, fluff—you know, all the girly stuff. Piece after piece I try them on and stand in front of my mirror. I ask myself, "Do I exist here? Is there space for me to breathe?" *No this one isn't right, my boobs are too booby. This one has my waist too pinched, my ass too present. This one screams GIRL* whatever the fuck that means. I rip them off one by one and throw them on the floor.

"I'm not sure who I am but she is not it," I whisper.

I've always felt more comfortable in boxers, tee-shirts-n-baggy, formless clothes. My stepmom judged me when I chose oversized jeans made for *boys* over the dresses she wanted me to wear. But, until my body differentiated me from them, I spent my time hanging with the boys. That's when I chose to wear skinny grey Pacsun jeans that emphasized my ass with thongs peeking out, low cut shirts and pushup bras, just to keep them near me. The boys. And really, the girls. No one wants to be friends with someone different when you're 12. No one wants to be different in middle school.

I find a large black garbage bag and shove the clothes in. Not quite ready to trash them, I throw them in the trunk of my car as an attempt to forget about them. As weeks turn to months, the bags double, triple, they take over my car.

***

I start to refer to myself as they in my head. I wear my boyfriend's clothes and almost cum when he peels his boxers off me, mouth moving towards my cunt. I spend my alone time reading posts by other queer folks questioning their gender and reveling in their transitions. I tease the topic to my partner, my mother, my friends, just to see their reactions. Calculating how big of a risk it would be to jump off the cliff and scream, "I am not a woman!"

My sibling comes out to me and my partner as nonbinary, and I feel hope. Hope in their bravery, hope in my partner's ability to support me in my truth, and hope in my ability to do the same. Hope I can embrace change without losing those I love. Those I think I need, especially him.

I have a fear that letting go of the things that attach me to my femininity, my perceived womanhood or whatever, will cause those I love to leave me. Or, that I would have to leave them. Put them in their own black bag, tie it up, and never look back. Maybe even set them on fire.

I tell him, "I'm not sure what I am, but I know I am not a woman. While I figure it out, I'd like it if you use they/them pronouns for me." Two weeks later, I break up with him. His lack of compassion in this request highlighted his lack of understanding of me as a whole. His panic about what my trans identity say's about him being my lover shows me once and for all that he loves me in boxes I no longer wish to squish myself into.

I put the boxes in the trash with all the clothes and shoes and 10 year old eyeshadow never worn. I let go of my hope in him.

I hold myself.

***

Before ever questioning my gender, I said: I am dee. In college: dirty dee. On stage: dee and the sunny saps. In friendships: dee. Partnerships: dee baby. The only people I didn't correct was my family. When they asked about it, I'd say, "Oh, it's just short for [redacted]—you do what you're comfortable with."

Now, after 8 years of:

Me: "Hi I am dee." Person: "Dean?"

Me: "Dee—like the letter but with two e's" Person: "Oh!"

I realize, I kinda like it. That my body responds openly to it. I realize in dreamland, I *am* Dean.

Me to me in my head looking in the mirror at the end of my bed: good morning Dean. Me to my friends: Dee is now short for Dean.

Me to the world: I am Dean.

I put that three syllable name my father gave me into the giant black bags full of my baggage.

***

I like to sit there naked in front of the mirror in the morning light and look at the lines and shapes my body makes. I trace my fingers over my soft skin, admiring him. This boy I am becoming. This boy who was in hiding, behind my hips, my clit, my tits. I press down on my tits and imagine they aren't there. I fantasize about what it would be like to liberate myself from them. No doctors. No anesthesia. No paperwork. No money. Just me, my body, a machete, and the earth.

My machete has a blue handle with white swirls like wind dancing around it. She fits perfectly in my grasp. Her name is Luna. She brings light to all of my shadows. We're in the woods under the cloak of a great willow. The stars are vibrant above us. The air is warm and humid. Sweat forms and drips down my forehead, torso, and legs. I feel alive when I sweat. My mirror rests on the base of the willow. Candles are lit around us in a circle; Luna, the willow and I.

I lay Luna on the earth and dance for her, the willow, the stars, for myself. I cover my arms, legs, neck, and torso in dirt and pray. On my knees, I grab Luna, and place her blade to my skin. I take four deep breaths.

Inhale: belly, ribs, chest. Exhale: chest, ribs, belly. Repeat.

With ease, and very little pain, I chop my tits off. The left and then the right; two swift strokes. My blood drips on the earth. My blood covers Luna. My blood covers me.

I dig a hole at the base of the willow and bury them at the roots of her. I cover them with fresh dirt, flowers, and tears. I let my blood drip from my chest to the dirt; christening us. She thanks me. I thank her.

"We're blood siblings now," I whisper.

I blow out the candles. I kiss the dirt. I dig my toes into the earth and stand. I stretch my arms over my head and breathe. I place my hands on my chest, sealing my wounds. I cover my body in a blue silk cloak. Smiling, I turn and walk back down the path from the willow to my bed, a new boy.

Finally free.

—**Dean Jones** (he/they)

Eileithyia

Eileithyia the bringer   goddess of birth and labor
blonde ringleted child   who pulled my hair
my friend my double   we were wicked sprites

our eyes arrest   in photographs   our parents doting   our friends
envious we were inseparable   we were a sacred cave

It was night   a knock at the door
I hid my treasures   crouched behind sofa cushions

Eileithyia's mother crying   kneeling on our doorstep
My father firmly shaking his head   then handing her a plastic bag of powder

We had come from caves   I wasn't allowed in your home
Your bell was broken so I'd pelt   your window with gravel bits
Dream of climbing up your fire Escape desire so palpable

        Myth says you are the Mother of Eros
        You were the mother of mine

Before I understood the war of misogyny
      I battled my   own blood for understanding

I fought and bled for answers   I slept with all my ancestors
and killed the dreams between   my legs how the antlers
char when war consumes

I took war into my mouth and   spat wrath in a
cataclysm of ash my   organisms subsumed in it

Mother of Eros Mother of Ash
We bled from sea to sea

Eileithyia warrior of the coy and fecund daughter of screams
I sublimated   my desire   in shopping malls & in the schoolyard

In wood-paneled basements   in suburban rec rooms
      in the sprawl of the casual   i adopted to pretend myself expansive
When making out with the drummer the bassist the drummer again the singer the singer the singers

I learned to loathe my kind so early i breathed it in like a costume i could not take off
The holiday tantrums and trauma headaches of eros in my young mouth
A cunt I could not fathom for its endless spun of mortal vigor
The death cycle of skin under the fluorescents skins in the dark deathbed room skins sagged ungraceful
and exhausted the black circle where I do not forgive you

Mother in Caves   Mother Limestone
        Mother of Carbon   Mother of Magma

—**Melissa Eleftherion** (she/they)

Peasant Song

We'll have our will in the woods
The waters and meadows
Which we walk in where will
O' the wisps unhide their light
Like fireflies, the binding ties
To an omen in blue, we gather
Mugwort and lavender lush
Rub rose petals into our wings.

In the summer we eat
Squash blossoms and berries
Ghostpipe bow, mycelium whisper
Careful signals underground.

Marching through the milkweed for monarchs
Around the lake and rooted along the river
Which needs rain

We plait leaves
Into an ephemeral crown,
Pat them down.

—**L. Noelle McLaughlin** (she/her)

Cave Song

On this nonimaginary number of a day
I thirteen my way into an ice cave,
Carved like cake, frosted and further on
Goldthread and gold leaf,
Black spruce and bird truce,
Mountain ash and also
An elder hostel for bats.

It's like a wedding in that way,
This mountain which I walk in,
This wet veil and inhale and conditioned responses
Of animals and air.

The old cement factories are cemeteries
Of propped up monolithic walls
And rusted out machineries.

In the summers a small woman
Brings big wheelbarrows full of flowers
To drape across the openings.

A platter of pinecones and blackberries with
Tablature scratched into the seeds,
Squat pines gather around to drink the dew.

—**L. Noelle McLaughlin** (she/her)

Eulogy of Amends

on a dark
winter night
my sister
was dying

but wait
it's more
complicated
than that

for my
first twenty
years she
was my brother

the shock
was so great
and the times
were afraid

we mistreated
my sister
and blamed
her poor health

but she
survived us
in her anger
estranged

secretly
I helped
with
her housing

while separating
from those
who could
not accept

but her years
of abuse
left
concrete distrust

we never talked
except
once
on the bus

one night
her landlord
sent me
a text

the ambulance
had come
and
gone

my sister's
partner answered
a bedside phone
in ER

and hung up
on me
and my
family of origin

so I cried
alone on
a dark winter
night

as my sister
died
and her partner
stood vigil

for this act
I will be
punished unto
death

who is my
mother, my father
my brother
my sister

—**L. Lois** (she/her)

First published by Zoetic Press

I Remember, I Thought, I Know

I remember I met Mark when I was eighteen and vacationing on a lake. We were the same age—I had thought. I remember wanting to kiss him, the first man I'd ever wanted to kiss. I hoped he wanted to kiss me too. I remember a particularly quiet summer night when he told me his story. How he had been blessed with eternal youth. I remember he told me he was actually hundreds of years old. I didn't want to kiss him after that.

I thought I saw Mark when I was twenty-three and touring Mammoth Cave National Park. A stranger on the tour group had joked about how old the caves were. I thought he had said, "You should have seen them back in the day." But he was younger than me, so he couldn't have said that. I thought I recognized his voice, his hair. But that was silly, at least at the time.

I know I heard Mark when I was thirty-eight and watching a parade go by. He had the same voice from the lake and Mammoth Cave. I know he sat right behind me, watching the parade and talking in my ear. "I never thought I'd see the day where people like us could just...be." I know he was sad. I didn't turn to look at him, but I gave him the flag I had been holding.

I hoped I wouldn't find Mark on the internet when I was sixty. So many Facebook ads claiming to have found "A Man Who Learned the Secret to Eternal Youth." I hoped the world hadn't found him and learned his secret. They were always just phony skincare routines. I hoped that Mark would stay hidden forever. Well, hidden to everyone except me.

I said goodbye to Mark when I was eighty-three. This would be the last time I ever saw or spoke to him again. I said goodbye to that same voice and hair from the lake, the cave, and the parade. The years had worn on him. I said goodbye to his story and his secrets. "You say you don't age, yet it seems you've aged a lifetime whenever I see you."

Mark laughed. Apparently in all his years, he'd never heard that before. Mark laughed, and I felt myself laughing too. "Well if you ask me," he said, "you haven't aged a day since I met you." Mark laughed, and for a moment we were the same. Eternally youthful even if only for a moment.

—**Chase Olsen** (he/him)

elegant g's

I'm walking down the street crunching the leaves
under my feet and I pass by the barber shop elegant g's

I let out a wistful sigh—this is the place I long
to go inside—I'd tell them to cut my hair as short

as they'd like—*you can do anything you want*
that makes me look gentlemanly—

and the irony because in my deepest fantasy
that's how I look already & they say—

let's give you a close shave and a clean cut—
nothing to do but sharpen those edges up

and after the trim, I come out looking prim
and proper and shockingly—if you can believe it—

a few inches taller & they've managed to shave
down all my soft curves so that I'm jagged

angular & I use the shop window as a mirror
and gaze intently at the rugged handsomeness

I see before me—*if only if only*—the tut tut
of a stranger's heels behind me snaps me back to reality

—**Alexandra Servey** (they/them)

Which Home – Kathleen Baker (she/her)

Lemon, Rosemary, Salt: An Evocation for Eric

"If you don't stand for something you will fall for anything."— *Gordon A. Eadie*

All I know is that those who don't remember themselves when they encounter a challenge are doomed to become someone else.

It began with a signature. My husband, Eric, insisted that he should sign everything in his name because it just "felt steadier". I thought about my good credit score, my name on the will that gave us this opportunity in the first place, and even my willingness to contribute. I should have been the name on the dotted line. He seemed to brush it away, and I felt compelled to do the same, as I was sure his intentions were fine, and really, *who could it hurt*?

The deed in question was the rights and belongings of my late parents' estate, who had spent their lives in intimacy and isolation but had still decided to leave their only child their possessions. They had a beloved gated farmhouse in Louisiana, surrounded by marshlands and adjacent to a private cemetery. As a kid I was too scared of the surrounding fog to even explore the twists and turns of what remained of other people's lives in the graveyard. I knew now that the fog, that seemed to live and breathe as normally as I did, was just a side effect of the cool marsh water and the humidity of the air colliding.

"Do you think any extra maintenance comes with the graveyard?" Eric asked me as we drove through the gravel and gates.

"Maybe, I could take care of it, work in it. I'm not setting foot there until daylight at least."

"Honey this isn't like the *work* you did back home." He seemed to shrug and pulled the car up to the doors, where some boxes already seemed straggled and opened. The gardener my parents hired had begun packing some things up and now there was a maze of half open boxes lining the halls.

"We meet with the realtor to decide if this place is even worth keeping tomorrow." I reminded him, to which he just nodded and put the car in park. "Any thoughts?"

That was the thing about Eric, he needed a little push sometimes to really define what his mind was working on.

"Sure. That sounds good."

The house was 100 years old, almost to the day, and the fine polished floorboards and nick free wallpaper were the product of my father's careful obsession. When walking through the house, I see him sometimes. I think of the times where he seems so clear. He was happy. He was proud. We aren't fighting. My father wears a ball-cap that's probably younger than me but looks so old that I mistake it for an antique. He wore sneakers I bought him for Christmas and he helped me set up my books on my desk.

My mother was distant most times in the memories I have of her, but she's there. She wore her hair in a tight barrette, silky black and smooth and tightened up on her head. When I moved into college, she rubbed salt and rosemary and lemon juice on my door to ward off bad spirits. She scoffs when my roommate asks what she's doing and says she should be thankful someone was taking precautions in a building as old as ours.

They don't talk about the house, they never mentioned why I can never go into the attic, where we store memories we can never retrieve. Eric probably remembers them just as fondly. He has little memory of them, as they never seemed to even leave to come see us. We always came down here to Louisiana. The first night we spend in the house, changing lightbulb after lightbulb, seemingly fried up when a breaker tripped. Eric packs up books, journals, candelabras and old dishes. I do our laundry and clean the guest room sheets.

That night I reach for Eric late, finding a cold spot on the bed where he should be. I lean my head over and find his glasses on his nightstand. He can't see without his glasses; can't see a thing.

My head drifts to the window, where the cool air blows the curtains about in an unsettling motion. Eric is there, watching the world below us on the lawn. I hear a rolling knock above me, light and small and steady: *thrum, thrum, thrum*. I'm sent back to my childhood, when my parents said to never leave the bed at night, no matter what I heard. My eyes close heavily, not by my own will, and I drift off to sleep.

But that fucked with me. The throttle and *thrum, thrum, thrum* of the attic seemed to be silent to him. The next morning, he doesn't remember getting up, but swears he has the strangest dream of a boat sailing offshore. Around lunchtime I hear whistling from the graveyard and pull curtains back to see the fog moving in. I mention it to Eric and he says it had to be a native bird calling out. I don't tell him I've never seen another living thing here for as long as I've lived.

That night I light candles, humming as my mother used to do when she set them out, carefully putting thought and promise into each one. She then sprinkled herbs beneath the attic, lemon zest, salt, and rosemary, then slept peacefully away. My father checked each doorknob, made of ironwood, and locked them all carefully. The lights go off, the candles burn out, and the attic stays silent.

I am so focused on our daily routine, making sure the house is tidy and all our work at getting it ready to sell or keep or tear down is not for nothing that I forget about Eric sometimes. I notice him sleepwalking at night, first to the window, then to the stairs, then with the front door wide open. He stands there, doorway wide agape like the jaws of a monster—the attic, its heart. He just stares, the cool wind numbing his fingers and toes and setting his jaw firm against his skin. He always comes back to bed. I always ask him how he slept, and he pushes me away each time. I'm starting to become exhausted with just empathizing with him.

I ask him in the morning if he believes in ghosts as we walk by the graveyard. He says in all honesty he doesn't, he thinks that people are just naturally scared. The fog from the marsh clouds his glasses that evening, and he takes them off repeatedly to clear them. The headstones are moistened from condensation and they sweat in the Louisiana evening. It somehow gets so cold here at night, colder than I remember, and I wonder if their marbled perspiration freezes them in place, or if instead they awaken and the corpses walk amongst us all. We pass the headstones of my parents, new and neat, with fresh Louisiana moss dangling over their markers.

"Do you believe in *anything*?" I ask him again as we pass a headstone whose flowers have shriveled up—black and tan and mildew infested. I don't dare move them.

He shrugs. He usually does just shrug, especially if it's about something *important*. "No. I just don't believe in anything I can't see, I guess. I've never had a reason to."

I thought about the graveyard, and how I didn't have to believe or see anything to know that it was wrong. It didn't seem to pull at him like it pulled at me, at least not during the day. During the night he got restless.

At night I watched him as we readied for bed, drinking tap water from the kitchen sink and staring out the window. He seems fixated on something beyond the fog, by the graveyard, but stays silent when I come to see. There is nothing there. Just fog. I look up at him in question, but he shakes it off. "You're being ridiculous with all that salt."

I do my nightly protection ritual and it keeps me calm. Eric scoffs at me as I sprinkle the herbs by the attic, by the door, the bedroom, in my tea, and by the fireplace. He says I act like a marsh witch in the bayou, cursing and drumming up hexes as I pad around the house letting them fall through my fingers: *thrush, thrush, ksshh*. They scatter like a collapse of snow down a mountain, fanning the wood beneath me. I finish my tea and climb into bed, watching as Eric's mug grows cold.

I tell him not to leave the house at night, but say it's because the lights outside are broken, not because I'm scared if he goes to the graveyard that calls to him, he may never come back. He says he never gets up at night and wouldn't think of it anyways, and I can see behind his eyes that he doubts me and my worries. He mumbles under his breath when I start to protest his disbelief again, but I stop as soon as his muffled grunts subside. That night I lock the doors, tight, more to keep him in than anything out. I hope he hears the throttle and *thrum* of the attic as we drift off.

We decide what to do about the attic in the morning; it must be one of us. He volunteers, rolling his eyes at my jitters. He has never believed in anything but dirt and rock and earth, anything and everything he can see and touch. He laughs at me. He grabs a ladder and ventures up, cockily remarking that attics were only alive in horror movies. He is silent for a while, sifting through papers and boxes, marking them here and there. I don't notice the sliding maple door close; I don't hear him for a while. He comes back down, a small stripe of blood poking out from his shirt. He says he must have scraped himself and brushes it off.

That was his last chance. I plead for him to tell me what happened in the attic—or what he sees in the graveyard—but he assures me with an eye roll that there is nothing to talk about. My heart stings because of his scoffing. Can he not see the mud on his shoes, the living fog as it swirls around the graveyard? Does he not remember anything about the dreams he has? His nocturnal pastimes must have some effect on him, or is he just that stupid? He sees me standing with my jaw set and *laughs*. He actually laughs.

"Look if that's what you want, I'll drink some of your fucking tea before bed. Will that make all this go away? Jesus."

He thinks I nag him. He thinks I should be gentler, dote on him after he's worked, give him attention when he hasn't said a word to me all day. He wants me to do my nightly rituals when he isn't there. *He wants me to disappear completely.*

I decide to make him a special blend that night. During dinner he watches me pour the tea into his cup and shakes his head with a smile. "My wife, the wicked witch of the bayou."

He drinks it with a grimace, but seems to power through, nonetheless. He finishes two cups before retiring with a third. He says after the second that the hot drink really grows on him. He makes fun of me, saying that this must be a bad batch. I sip my own tea, mercilessly.

He showers and readies himself for bed once again, early in the afternoon. I make him soup and tea, but he has neither. He falls asleep at dusk as I read in the study, silent and restful. I notice he is still asleep when I get dressed after my tea and I hear him snoring. His teacup is empty, the remains of the blend of grave dirt and sugar swirled at the bottom. I wonder how long it will take tonight, but I know that I have done all I can.

That night I stay awake, book in hand, and I wake up to see him traveling down the lawn. Glasses still on the nightstand, footsteps leaving no track. By the pricking of my scorned thumb, something wicked this way comes, fucker.

—**Izabella Harvey** (she/her)

Flowers for the Dead

So much talk of flowers these days, as if there weren't so many dead. You will say again the as- sumption to be made, as if I haven't made it: flowers for a dead love. I will tell you something now: all of it was your imagination. Believe you me, the dead are dead and accept no flowers. I have given you every flower imaginable, a love for you, alive for you, and yet you resurface along with the dead. Forgive the honest interval, you say, I must, for what is love without the love birds finding roadkill in the road ahead. If you don't know how to love, then don't, I say. If we must be honest, I am tired, that is my side of the bed you impede on, floating in the air with the words airborne, lethal. I give no sympathy cards for the dead, no flowers too. Only my sympathy, only the flowers of my face. And yet again we stride so causally within our house of metaphor. If the dead come back, they come to us in forms we can never fathom, but only to give us a vision of what it might be were we to resurface with them. As if a poem with no reversal. As if they cannot come back to tell us what might be in the vision. As if you could ever fathom the dead flowers of my face. It is I who have built a card stock house of shame, only I who must live in it. I, who have no sympathy, who show no remorse, who show no pain when words are twisted in the air that car- ries disease to my side of the bed. I am tired, of this undying love, honest prayers unanswered and inherently unreciprocated, from those who don't know how to love even a flower. In the road ahead, carry this, instead: a love of birds, not roadkill, who talk but do not hear, who answer with- out listening. Forgive the interjection of the bird. Only that it has a message as it pollinates the flower: smell it, the bird or the flower, and you will smell the pungent hour of an air with an af- tertaste. It is that aftertaste, in the air the moment someone dies, that remains. I accept no flower. You are dead to me. Believe you me. The lingering look was imagined. All of it was of the poiso- nous air: the flower, the bird, the pollination into the stem's blood stream. And poisonous talk. As if there weren't so many dead. As if there weren't so many flowers.

—**Angela Gabrielle Fabunan** (she/her)

R.I.P

A photo in shreds, my bedroom
floor its' final resting place

haphazard trail from bin to door
body parts peppered with beer
cigs and gin

shreds scatter down like
falling snow, eyes obliterate
hands obliterate shoes obliterate
you

sore hands, blood stained fingers
no deterrent

rip, shred, scatter
rip, shred, scatter
rip, shred, scatter

obliterate eyes, obliterate hands,
obliterate pain, obliterate man, obliterate
you.

—**Joanne Le Grove** (she/her)

Memory Box

In sleep, I see sideways, underneath unfrozen water and
        egg-colored bedcovers, I toss and turn with eddy lines echo,
          wanting you to come to me like layers of

        photo paper, flaking like somber rainbow mica,
      your gazing compound eyeglass. You hover in, a dragonfly: as
a comb straightens your long hair, and latches onto curling knots.
I watch, wanting to float, to forget these
      accumulated entanglements.

We walk, together and towards each other, through
      jade dimming to greys—a fen adrift under powder sky,
        a funeral, a birthing house, a developing room. A photo lens
        twists over that last few feet,

And circles to pause at a hyperfocal
   distance, reaching through glowing
     foglight for flesh and wings,
        to find only clouded light.
        your eyes flash forever, from behind `
    lapis rims. I'm still, you hover, your hands another box of art,
     fingertips cradle the gift reel.

I had been waiting to develop all of it, in your hands,
      hunting the same roll of images—the single ocean, wood grain and
       champagne bubbles, organs flashing in an incinerator,
        Us with our second and infinite chances,
        That last quarter turn,

   memories reflecting, answering an invitation to a levitating future,
      —some now past, and some past now, some, negatives, A swish of out
breath, shapen clumsily into words, like
        "I love you", And "teapots".

In our time's care, this nymph Memory Box, had become
     no longer mine, Nor yours, and Not ours, nearly
      orphaned in our terminal gentleness, held between us like
       drying wings, Thinner than paper, stronger than stars.

Not vacant, not swirling, not stillborn.
Your eyeglasses honest to this optic surface, askew between
eyes and air, returned with this reel, these photos
—snow and hat brims, a dog now passed, waves on lakes and   creatures
from bodies of water larger than you had ever seen.

By the wand of your abdomen, your belly alights, light darts through
pinholes to land around you. your fingertips and mandibles open as
you push the box, reel inside, with every photo, every wingbeat,
to the space between us. Each nudge sinks haze,
humming movements of your body float in weighted evaporation

I look down, your jaw full and square, cheekbones holding
eyeglasses and photo lenses, I try to push the box back
into your soft hands,
"take them back, I already have my own world, and
I gave it to you. I want yours."

I waited, waiting for his, for Some second and third thing.
For us both to—Something else, Something undeveloped

You replied, glasses shifting, cradled by your face, a dragonfly before he strikes.
You put them back in my hand, tapping the film case thorax,
"this is where I've been living, for a long time now, in this box."

We gazed at how we had been weighed down by something so small as
shared memory, light as film, heavy as imagery, and
exposed the reel to raw light, the photos falling to vernal pools,
their colors running into each other and then back in to the water. The box's dark   unfurls,
Inside out,

naked to the water, Becoming emerald, undecided veneer.
We took hands and hovered out over the waves,
Climbing droplets of saved tears. Up, Ever up in little wingbeats,
to start over.

—**Fern** (they/them/she/her)

Santa Rosa – Kathy Bruce (she/her)

Therapy

Looking for a seam
For a way in, through and out
A safe pass to cross the veil between worlds

Too small to defend themselves
They sucked love from a poisoned teat
Weaned on vipers' milk
The bitter hiss
The coiled intensity
The never knowing
When they would strike

Throw these thoughts on the fire
One by one
Watch them catch light
Curl red around the edges
Wither to ash and embers
To cremated corpsed cinders

Whilst spirits witness
And smoke rises

Holy

—**Amanda Ball** (she/her)

Four Girls in a Two Person Tent

We are four girls in a two-person tent. Our legs tangle together. Our mothers don't allow any of us to shave above the knee yet, so most of the time we don't bother with below the knee at all. Our soft downy legs rub against each other like the soft side of the blanket.

The tent doesn't have a window—it's not that fancy. We keep the door open a little and mosquitoes are buzzing around, we slap each other every time we see one land, leaving little bloody kisses up and down our limbs. I wonder if I let my hands linger too long—

Scabby and sunburned. Part little girls, part Lolita.

We have gangly limbs and baby fat cheeks. Long Pre-Raphaelite hair that grows like weeds, and gives us power like swamp witches.

This is the summer. I will turn 15, but I am not 15 yet.

I hate camping. I never owned a sleeping bag and nobody wanted me to feel bad about being poor. So, we just brought the puffs and blankets from our twin beds and our bed pillows.

I even brought my *Kitty Cuddler*. A nasty misshaped stuffed cat on a little heart pillow. One of her eyes is smashed shut as if she has been hit. I got her when I was 7 for Valentine's Day and I have now had Kitty Cuddler for half my life.

I have known and loved these girls even longer than that.

Holly and I met when our moms did. They were two exhausted women who felt like ghosts. Just women in line at the supermarket. Bags under their eyes and terrible floral sundresses. They got to talking about *Days of Our Lives*, and Holly and I were just babies then, so I don't remember it, but I imagine our innocent doll eyes finding each other then. I imagine even as a baby I would have known that she would be the other half of my heart well into my 20's.

I met *little Missy* when her parents moved in down the street, they were French too, and my mother would spend hours finally speaking her language with a friend while smoking long brown cigarettes that smelled minty and earthy. They would tell secrets.

Missy and I took dance together. Two little ballerinas in stage makeup with hyper flexible legs. Sometimes our moms would be late picking us up from class, and we would watch the big kids—our heads pressed together on the other side of a two-way mirror. We thought we were looking at our future. We would chew on the ends of each other's long hair as if we were cats.

Sarah, I met when I was 10, when I was double digits and was no longer forced to exist in the childhood prison of my street. She was a 10-minute walk and another world away. Her older sister had a Ouija board, and her parents were never home. She had big brown eyes and a voice that sounded like a cartoon.

She was the cute one.

I didn't want to know which one I was, but that night while camping but not camping I realized I was the quiet one, the sad one.

I would be the one who stays. The one who doesn't move. The one that will stay in this tent forever, even though I hate camping.

It's Sarah's backyard, but it's Missy's tent.

We are drinking wine coolers and rum with diet Pepsi.

It's the middle of July and none of our moms have let us have anything except Slim Fast since school let out three long weeks ago. Twenty-one long and starving days.

Our mothers know that it is time that we become pretty.

They know it's time for us to attract skater boys and 24-year-old perverts who play in bands.

Slim Fast

Slim Fast

Slim Fast

I am not sure if my parents know where I am; this is the summer that we were never home. Night after night at someone else's house. Rarely mine.

My house had parents that never spoke to each other, bathroom faucets that we had to tie with strings to keep them from dripping, and a mom who stayed out all hours of the night. All this and somehow no booze to be stolen in the house.

Other houses had older siblings, HBO, and cabinets above the fridge that were never guarded. We ate chips and then ran around the block until all calories were burned.

It is not August yet.

July is still *this*.

July is this tent.

July is warm rum and tangled, soft legs.

By summer's end I will be 15, and I will wake up in the middle of the night, my mother hitting my father over and over again, trapped in some kind of waking and walking dream.

Trying to kill *him* but not him.

By the end of summer my mother will be sleeping on the porch, and Missy and Holly will have both gone off to camp—they will send me postcards filled with names I don't know, and come back with stories. Holly went to second base with a boy, and Missy went to third.

I stayed home. I went nowhere.

I have just stayed in this tent.

The most beautiful place to be when you hate camping.

—**Jennifer Anne Gordon** (she/they)

The Author Uses Too Many Metaphors in This One

I am a toothy maw,
a mosh pit full of
swinging arms &
kicking legs.

Somewhere, lives a
picture of me with
a broken rib & a smile,
stranded at a concert venue
just outside of Boston.
I am the happiest there
that I have ever been.

I am a taxi cab,
a yellow checkered chariot
pulled along by
nicotine addictions &
one too many all-nighters.

Over time I learned to
love the color of my hair
but I still go back and look
at the memories of
when I was everyone's
favorite bottle blonde.

I am a collapsing star,
a jumbled mess of infinite chaos
falling inward on itself
& reaching out for light.

Even when I can't think of things to write,
I can always find a way
to paint over an old canvas.
I am nothing if not innovative.

—**Gabriel Noel** (he/him)

I'm Two Sizes Larger
  —with reference to "Cut Piece" by Yoko Ono 1965

you cut every last clothing tag
from my shrinking wardrobe
I've outgrown these blazers
always wanted to be bigger
like muscles like brawn in a suit
at a wedding with a brown leather belt
and oxfords but I am prematurely menopausal
which is more tummy–less
non-binary person with shoulders
ovaries I cannot escape—the sink of you
a crater at the edge of the bed
while you describe AI as missing its
edges in the same but opposite way
dreams blur the obstacles we might
otherwise bump into naturally
daydreaming except without permission

anyway I remember Yoko Ono
as she sat torn on the gallery floor
the violence of cutting
someone's clothing with permission

I bump into the transformation of my body
naturally like a slow blink
I know you are here to cut away
the smaller sizes from my beloved
articles of clothing but I fear
it's up to me to accept the obstacles
to speak more kindly about labels
to blur the violence into a divine act of love

            —Chelsie Blair Nunn (they/them)

You Can't Build a House on an Earthquake

There is no transience, no motion, in the expectation of monogamy. How habitual, to keep a heart in a box & not have to keep winning it. To be possessed, to be preserved, as if the passing of time is external to this partnership. Partners in *what*, I want to ask. Sitting beside each other on the bed? Neck kisses? Companionship? Stagnancy?

My soul is a river & I want to run with it. My world & I, we are ever-changing. I want to sink my teeth into everything I want you to sink your teeth into me but you're afraid of causing pain & I think that is cowardly. I keep trying to tell you who I am but you think you know me. I don't want to be comfortable, I want to be challenging. Sometimes I fantasise about you getting angry just for a change of scene. Everything is too soft & I have never been one to stay.

Does one kiss make a cage—like I am your pet woman & you are my pet boy? If I am yours what will you do with me? Show me to your friends? Show me to your mother? Run your fingers down the back of my neck? Hold me? Listen to me yap & not say anything back like we don't speak the same language?

It's so quiet & I'm tired of everything being the same all the time. I am not the same in autumn as I was in summer. You've got new friends & I don't like them. I've got new longing & it's pulling me away. I can remember when I stopped writing love poems. I can remember when it changed. You look at me & only see my face. Our foundation is shaking. Baby, you can't build a house on an earthquake.

—**Devon Webb** (she/her)

slow, deliberate.

i walk back onto the front porch with my chin up,
flames licking up the grass and the weeds behind me.
there is fire in my stomach and in my mouth and in my front garden.
this evening
i left all the lies i've ever told in a heap on the lawn,
lit a match and tossed it.
saw the spark scramble for certainty until it found something sturdy to catch on to. then,
watched the embers grasp at the darkening twilight from my front porch.
the match is still hot, so
i light a cigarette.
i think about how,
before i lit the lies up,
i tied a note to the kindling in the front yard with god's name on the envelope.
in the letter i didn't ask for forgiveness but i did ask for something—
for something
slow, deliberate.
flames don't travel as fast as you think they do.
the lies burn slow and so do i and so does the cigarette,
but soon enough
the lies are gone
and i'm left smoking on an empty porch,
staring out at the scorched remains of my front grass.
i see the figure of all the things i've ever wanted
drifting into form in the curling smoke.
and all of a sudden,
i'm not
waiting on a reply from the sky;
i put out the cigarette
and resolve to build the world myself.

—**Katie Barlow** (she/her)

Untitled – Maya Collins (she/her)

Satan Sucker Goes to Manhattan
—*after Weekend Nachos*

romance of the
fist to
fist to
    face.   sexual. nationalism. so-called love. blood runs

thin here. i kiss him cuz he's
     him.

i don't need our hands to be organized in a right way. cuz i've got all left limbs &
it's more "exotic" to fuck

    let alone fuck
    a faggot. a white ant buries its bald
    head in the mud. it feels
    wrong but so do the right

things.
we kiss crosses hung
by nooses. it's bdsm. it's
at its finest. it's

    numb to the touch. cuz we hate to love living things or things like
    people. people
    like us

        we just don't require a correct series
of method. we just don't need them.

—**Liam Strong** (they/them)

depression hits

after retching all night and half a day
a virus rather than drink this time
yes, it's been eighteen months
and
today i remembered what it felt like
to sweat through the sheets
and give away my remains to the half-filled bin
to want oblivion so much
it hurts to wake
like when i googled
heft only to find rot
while trying to write
a poem about my breasts
what lies underneath their
heart, rot which affects beets
imagine their dirty heart beats
and bleeding skin under the
surface of the ground, as i try
to pull myself out of the covers
walk downstairs to find the mess
on another day i might find gratitude in
dishes in the sink and his small
clothes scattered in piles around the house
the dog hair in the carpet and what the fuck
is that stain on the couch—
morning heaviness
morning heft
i heave myself into newness
hoping i come back tomorrow
hoping this rot hasn't yet reached my heart

—**Ashley Howell Bunn** (she/they)

My Life with Men in Cars

5/3/2024

2002 Buick LeSabre

The day that I knew I hated my boyfriend the way I hated my father was on Easter Sunday. It was 2016—the year I graduated high school, the year he graduated college, and the year America imploded on itself in a way we had never seen before—at least not this online. Perhaps it was the election, perhaps it was Pokemon Go, perhaps it was the death of David Bowie or the thousands of other things that happened during that godforsaken year. Whatever it was, I was in his white 2002 Buick, the coins dirty yet neatly stacked in the beige center console, his ex-girlfriend's play program from 2012 tucked away in the glove compartment, and my tears streaming steadily down my face as they had the month after we started dating. On my way to his house in my mom's silver 2006 Chevy Cobalt that was rusting away underneath and smelled of Sonoma 100's, I saw a woman hit a guardrail and spin out, driving down King's Creek Road like it never happened. It felt like she and I were about to have the same day.

"Why aren't you taking your medication?" He said—his green eyes could have been black or purple or orange and I wouldn't have noticed—his face set sternly, a man and a statue becoming the same thing in that moment.

I was fresh off of a suicide attempt that January—the day I tried to drown myself in my bathtub for the third time was my best friend's birthday, and it seemed as if I was ruining every close relationship in my life. I feign forgetfulness in my mind's eye, my memory's tomb, but really, I was mentally unwell, nearing narcissism if not already there, and begging for the attention I had been starved of my entire life. I was, by all accounts, a product of my terrible upbringing, the bastard child of two people who hated each other and themselves, which oftentimes turned into hating me. I was the textbook only child—needy, demanding, vexing to my peers and superiors, and breaking as many social boundaries as I could in order to feel like I existed in some way that was unique to all of the people I went to high school with. I didn't care about how badly, how annoyingly, or how wrongly I did the things I did for attention—all I knew in my 18-year-old brain is that I could not fade into the background like my parents had. Whatever I did, no matter how I did it or why I did it, was to make myself seen. To make myself known. To not become my dead and forgotten ancestors—both pairs of grandparents, an aunt, many uncles, and too many cousins to count.

"I don't fucking *know*," I told him, as I had told him before and would tell him for five miserable years later. He had me in the palm of his hand and he knew it—his thing, he thought, forever.

Men love power, and men love the control that power gives them even more. Especially when it involves an impressionable, broken, and severely mentally ill teenager with an ego that needed to be humbled the same way I needed a semblance of self-identity, self-esteem, and a different family entirely.

My destiny seemed to burn itself into the engine of his car, the whirring of the 14-year-old engine that would transform into a Beamer just a few short years later. Rowan's post-grad job as an engineer paid well—better than anyone I had personally known—and his main goal in life was to become a landlord, buy a Lamborghini, and become so financially comfortable that he could likely retire before the age of 40.

My dream was to make it to college. And when I got there, I was an English major, dating an engineer, the only dream I held as firmly as Rowan's: just having the opportunity to even be there in the first place.

My tears became the moment and I put my head into my hands, my box-black dyed hair splitting at the very seams and begging for anything other than V05 and maybe even a decent haircut I couldn't afford. My mascara turned into badly kept roads, running down the length of my face. Rowan was really all that I had—I had spent weekends down in Morgantown visiting him during his senior year at West Virginia University, giving up the freedom of my senior year to spend his last hurrahs with him. He had tried to convince me to transfer from my high school in Weirton, an hour and a half away, to Morgantown High School, where I could escape the abusive situation of my father's alcoholism and my mother's absence and feel what it felt like to be loved. It seemed nice, but it was a retrospective hellscape—he made me eggs that were always too burnt, he gave me opioids from his wisdom tooth prescription and alcohol I couldn't yet purchase for myself, and the sex was so underwhelming that by the time we had been dating for two years we stopped having it altogether. I loved him, because he was there. I loved him because there was no one else on this earth in 2016 who seemed to share the same sentiment, regardless of how ridiculous or self-inflated or annoying that is to admit to my word processor as I type this. I loved him because I barely knew him and he seemed to know everything about me.

I was a shell of myself. And my relationship showed it.

His hands grabbed the steering wheel and I didn't know what to think, because I never really did when it came to communicating conflict with other people. I was so scared of the idea of him leaving me that I was willing to do anything and everything to get him to stay, even if that meant remaining in a relationship that should have ended after 6 months and certainly shouldn't have lasted for five years. Rowan loved the silent treatment—he loved the power of being bigger, mentally and intellectually and physically, than the person standing in front of him. Even if it was his mom. Even if it was his sister. Even, and especially if, it was his girlfriend. He loved to turn his Playstation off during Death Souls when he was about to lose, and his favorite hobby was boycotting restaurants that served him the wrong food or charged him too much. Without his mundane sense of control over the things in his life that had wronged him, he felt as powerless as I was born to feel.

I stared at the floor, the windshield caked in wedding white bird shit, the glove compartment that held the Beauty and the Beast playbill starring a girl I had never met but was eerily similar to.

Both only children, both eventually completing their PhD before their 30th birthday, both eventually driving foreign Polly Pocket cars with their red, curly hair flying out the windows and into the rare air of remembrance. We were, in many instances, a mirror of each other moving through the confusing plane of time, space, and romance.

I sniffled at the thought of her. I wondered if she ever did the same with me.

I knew that Rowan cared deeply for me, despite his overbearing quest for domineering manhood and his anger and control issues. I knew, and still know, that he was a deeply afflicted person who found it hard to romantically connect with another person. I knew that while he was flawed, I was even more so, which was what made our relationship so impossible to exist comfortably within. I felt too deeply and idealistically about the world I was just about to enter—he felt too realistically and logically about the world he already knew something about. We were, in many ways, two people who had just kind of fallen into a relationship with what seemed like no way out—too deeply enmeshed, too brazenly stubborn in different directions, and too proud to admit that our relationship had been failing for most of the time we were both in it.

The car was hot in the parking lot across from his parents' home, where most of our fights usually occurred. I wondered how many people saw us in that Buick, one face stern and the other tear-stained. I wondered if they knew what we both knew but refused to admit for half a decade after—and I wondered if they had ever faced a similar situation. Like they were trapped with someone that should have made sense, but didn't in the moments it mattered. Like they felt their entire life folded out in front of them—the financial security, the family they never had, the house with the kids and the stainless steel appliances. Like it all seemed like it should make sense, like it should feel right, like it should feel like fate—but it never did. It instead always felt like a peach pitted stomach and another conversation buried underneath the dirty but clean coins and that goddamned playbill.

I am trying to write kindly about this moment. I am trying to remember the good times we shared—the laughs, the emotional upheavals always on my end, his thoughtfulness and his gifts and the time and care and compassion he gave to me when I needed it the most. I think of him carrying me out of the hospital in grippy socks in January, though I also remember him yelling at me for slamming his car door to the Buick when I saw the neighbor who sexually abused me in Kroger, his coffee and Black n' Mild stained breath leaning closely to my ear and saying "Hello". But when I think of that car, in that parking lot, this time and the time before and the thousands of times after, I get sick to my stomach. I want to vomit—I want to erase them from my mind, the time we shared, the Christmases his father caught on camcorder, the kinship I found in them—all of it. I want to take the mistakes that I made more than he did and I want to burn them to the ground. I want to take my regret and smash the glass into that very parking lot and walk on the glass shards afterwards. I want to stop feeling bad about writing about this moment, the pinnacle of many moments we shared, and I want to be able to tell the truth as I see it. Even now, after admitting this all to you, I find it impossible to not give you purple prose and deliver a narrative that is fair to the both of us.

The conversation we had on Easter Sunday in 2016 is less full of dialogue and more full of feeling—his loss of control of me, his paper doll girlfriend who wore clothes that were too tight and talked so loudly it embarrassed him so much that it began to embarrass me. This moment in that car reminds me of all of the other forlorn instances—the time in Dollar General when he told me I needed to stop being so kind to the people working because they might take it the wrong way. I think of when I smoked weed with my friends and he took away the Playstation he was letting me borrow to play Spyro as a punishment for going against his rules for me—no drugs except the ones I was prescribed, no cigarettes, and no friendships he deemed unfit. I think about all of the times my freshman year of college when Frank had to watch my sobbing, convulsing body turn snakelike as he yelled at me over the phone for going to a frat house, grinding on my gay friend at the club, or ignoring his calls when I wouldn't text him back quickly enough.

I try to convince myself that these five years of my life were a lesson in the making—that the control Rowan held over me was the control I desperately needed and wanted from my own father, who only took the time to yell at me over keeping crackers in my shoebox, terribly painted purple bedroom or stealing too many of his cigarettes. I think of Rowan as the parent that I never had—giving me the guide to life I was never given by my own parents. He cured my loneliness in a way that only an older boyfriend can—with relentless rules and moving goalposts, all under the guise of keeping me alive and well.

When we finally left the car that day and entered his parents' home, I wiped the tears and mascara away from my eyes and pretended that it was fine, that we were fine, and buried my sorrows deeply into his mother's greens that I still have dreams about. I also think of the mistakes that I made during our time together as I ate our Easter dinner together—the relentless and embarrassing stupidity he had front row seats for. I think of the time I unabashedly used his sister's nail polish that was sitting on the kitchen table, and how she told Josephine, and how Josephine told Emma, who told me four years later while we smoked weed at an overpass on a hiking trail in Pittsburgh. I think of how I fell in love with Sawyer, who wasn't into me until four years into our friendship, despite my falling completely and madly in love with him after he performed at a gig in our college's amphitheater, and how I had to hide it from Rowan for the last two years of our relationship and pretended that I wasn't so petrified of leaving him for someone else who wanted nothing to do with me. I think mostly of all of the times I lied because I was too scared to tell the truth, and how much of a coward that makes me, even still, and definitely always. Beyond a coward, even—a petrified liar who felt stuck, unseen, and unwanted by what would end up being the right person and wanted far too much from what ended up being the wrong person.

When I had tried to leave, I ended up coming back because there was nowhere else to go. The first time I tried to break it off with him, I called him screaming, vomiting, and begging for his body in my bed beside me. The second time, he promised changes that he somewhat kept and told me he would be a bigger part of my life with my friends in our duplex on the hill. While he let go of his grip on my neck, maybe even more so after he choked me so hard during sex that I passed out, I still didn't feel free enough to leave him. The other times, muddied by my mind's eye, involve him refusing to come and see me in Morgantown because his Beamer was too nice and my street was too sketchy. As my senior year of college approached and my undulation with Sawyer grew larger than the valleys of West Virginia where both of us came from, my hatred for Rowan that began that Easter Sunday grew larger and hotter and more daunting than I was prepared to admit.

So, I ate the greens, the ham, the mashed potatoes and laughed with Rowan's family at their kitchen table and pretended so hard to be a girl I wasn't that it felt like childhood dress-up. I became the girl I was supposed to be, or should have been, in order for his family to accept the fact that their son was a senior in college dating a high schooler who was four years older than their youngest son. And when his mother cleaned up dinner from that evening and scraped the plates into leftover dishes to put into the fridge for the foreseeable future, I thought of my own. I pondered the possibility of myself without Rowan—no more holidays, because my family stopped celebrating them years ago. No more recorded Christmases or family get-togethers or birthday parties at the same table I always pretended to be someone else at.

I thought of my life scraped into those Tupperware dishes, put onto a chilled shelf to be consumed at a later date until there was nothing left of me to eat.

I figured that maybe it was better to just rot away on those shelves instead.

—**Shan Cawley** (she/her)

Junk Drawer – Alexis Telyczka (she/her)

Shh... the Soft Gnaw

Often times
I am hungry and wandering
Back and forth in the house
Moisture sucked from my mouth
Burning acid in my stomach
Toes frozen and turning blue

What's something you see?
What's something you feel?

I smell premenstrual sweat
Warding men away
Rank odor that speaks without words

She cannot conceive this week or the next
Come back later when her face is more symmetrical

So I stay hungry and wandering
Waiting for
What exactly?
Thief of iron
To sit on my chest while I sleep
Knock wind from my lungs
And whisper my worst fears in my ear
While running fingers through my hair

Saying
Shh...at least now you know

Even though I don't

At least now it's over

Even though it's not

Thief of iron
Kisses my cheek
As the lack of oxygen
Makes my head pound

What do you see?
What do you feel?

I taste rot
Where his spit used to be on my tongue
I taste bile
Where his breath used to warm my neck

When he said *I love you*
I love you
You are so gorgeous
Before showering me with kisses like shrapnel on a sand dune
I may be pocked and scarred from the fall out
But each laceration felt like the softest eyelash
every time another fell onto my cheek
My wish was the same

Let him stay
Let him stay
Let him stay

—**Rowan Miller** (she/her)

Against Trypanophobia or Trans and Afraid of Needles

      (I don't remember if she really said "knife")
hold it like a pen—not a knife ↗   just that it was bloody
she told me the fifteen minutes
she squeezed me in between abortion
consultations & HRT follow-ups for
     ↘ (really it's GHAT in the medical community)
   more affirmed
those who were ~~older~~ and wiser than me
        sure I could even do it
I had braved the PPFA injection videos to be ~~sure~~
  (looking away when the needle went in)
but don't close your eyes

     less invasive)
subcutaneous sounded easier so Sunday
   belly fat needle
became ~~pinching~~ and ~~poking~~ day
and the code word for my condition
   (trans and afraid of needles)
because how does one convince the mind
to pierce the belly fat between my fingers?
    ↘ (pinched for half an hour already)
but don't close your eyes tender like a mushed flower stem

and yet it is so good
 I
~~you~~ wrenched out angered sobs to
   suffocating incapacity
silence the ~~debilitating hesitation~~
  (at a 45° angle)
to *insert the needle 3/8ᵗʰ of the way*
and I promise it won't hurt
      I   myself
  ↘ (except the time ~~you~~ poked ~~yourself~~)
but don't close your eyes and a bead of blood blossomed

—Wilfred Jensen (they/them)

Upbringing

We did not give permission to be brought forth. We never consented to be here, never came to the table to agree upon the terms of our upbringing, nor the names kissed upon our heads. We were brought up to be one version of ourselves, figments of mild imaginations. Appropriate, as in valuable, as in safe from harm. But they could only bring us so far. We grew into our own stories, imagined ourselves more true and wild. We began to set our own terms. We re-made ourselves—reached inside and discovered new names, not knowing exactly who we were becoming in the unbecoming of what was never true. Taking the words they gave us, the stories, and warnings, and rhymes we broke them down into sounds and began to sing a re-mix, a new song of ourselves. Slowly for some and suddenly for others, surprising anyone who was not paying attention, we brought forth our new selves, our new songs and symphonies and we offered our melodies to our mothers. We said, if you want to know me, just listen. And call me by my name.

—**Sara Triana** (she/her)

am i a girl or a god?

a bible still sits in the drawer of my nightstand
the same one i had read cover to cover last year
in search of a verse from our mother who art in heaven
! hallow be the dykes !
ones i kissed under flickering bulbs as the world grew dark
lights leave bedroom windows lonely and blind.

small beads of blood rain off my kneeling body
shoulders pressed into the ground where my lips grow dry from puddles
the reflection of yellow thread and black leather gleams
under stars suspended with veins in the sky
performing small, jolted dances—the puppeteer controls midnight
and there is a small wren hopping towards me
splashing water on my face
and pecking at the dirt in the roadside garden.

winter sheds to summer
and something around my feet is swaying
soothing senses where once i had begged
standing on a threshold of teeth at the front door of my father's home.

being a lesbian must be the best sin
or at the very least the gentlest tear i could put in the earth
that a beak carves a crescent through my heart
and soon i can stitch up my spine
it wasn't until i kissed a girl that i thought i could be a mother
that i found i am not a girl or a god but a failed version of both
and i can sew all the torn flesh of my life into one—
hold something and not feel a knife but a withering thorn painting blood across my stomach.

now that i have seen myself rationalizing through answers i never reached for
when my legs were stubby and my arms couldn't extend to the cupboard
here i lie
kissing water under evening eclipses
blinding myself from faces in windows
and taking breaths so that sometime maybe we could kiss once again.

—**Abigail Cain** (they/she)

92

when they won't call us by our names

That the world exists beyond
the names we are given, the names

we give our children, that language
is born of air, flows like a river,

is hands in a flutter like the wings
of whip-poor-wills who we call after

their vocalization, the wings
of swifts who prefer to stay

aloft instead of perch, the wings
of monarch butterflies

traveling from mountain forests
to swamp milkweed

behind the home where I live
in a world that loves us back.

—**Emily Carlson** (she/they)

BETELGEUSE

—A large old star that has left the main phase of its life

Most are green-blue like agave, lichen,
and auroras. Rorschach inkblots of leaky
blood vessels that are deeply photogenic.

They fight with one another to star in
my universe; asteroids and meteors
spiraling in concentric orbits.

Right here, on the back of my knee,
a luminous galaxy of pooled plasma,
from squeezing the stainless steel pole.

This one, a hazy eddy in my armpits from
free-styling like a rogue planet. Virgo and
Ursa congeal on lips no longer waxed.

For an hour each week in the studio, this
pole is mine, a silver veil in muted red light.
I lick her; clutch her with my inner thighs.

Here, I'm alive and beautiful enough.
My clots! My clusters! My cosmos! Oh,
how I grieve when you begin to fade.

—**Sherry Shahan** (she/her)

Love Song With an Apology

I won't bother you with preambles: I'm a difficult person to love.
I am reckless, antsy, ocean-deeply damaged. I cry as often as most people laugh,
cry at the way the sun comes through our partially open blinds,
at the burnt eggs on the pan; at nothing in particular, really. There must be a leak
in the pipeline between my heart & the world. Something missing in my
armour, if there ever was such a thing.
I cry & cry & cry & you,
—endless, saintly, you—hold it in your hands. & oh, what do I do?
What do I do with this wild floodgate, this untamed waterfall. This broken
bundle of infinite mistakes. I want to crawl towards you
on all fours. I want to say I'm sorry.
Sorry for the bloody fingers, the heavy red eyes, for the handful of pills I take
when I think you're not watching. Sorry my hands
are the heaviest thing you will ever carry.
But, God, if I love you—
& I do, I do—if I love you, no other weight
can ever get between that.

—**Dante Émile** (he/they)

Praying Backwards

I pray backwards.

"That's sacrilegious," Mama tells me when I get around to mentioning it, but how would she know? Mama's only a child herself, barely 25 years old. She still wears short dresses, her knees flashing at God as she sits in the pew chewing her gum, and I know the certainty will fade from her face as wrinkles start to stake their claim. I'll bring the topic up again when we're both older—she might feel differently—but somehow I never got around to it.

Saint Joan is the one who inspires me to start praying backwards. At school they make sure I know all about her: leading armies of men, wearing men's clothes, captured by men, questioned by men, and killed by men. At school they say there's nothing I can do, because it's "already happened." Joan was 19. I am only 7, and I want more for her. I send my prayers marching all the way back through time into her outstretched hand as she stands alone in that damp prison cell.

I'm 16 and I do it again.

I'm 26 and the prayers change. Everything changes. Sorry, Saint Joan.

Now I'm older still. I haven't thought of that lonely fighter in so long. Here, have one more. Perhaps the prayer of a dying old woman, standing on the edge of a crumbling world holds more weight than that of a child. Maybe together we can still change everything that's ever happened.

The nurse eyes me with distrust as she moves through the room, checking to make sure everything is where it belongs. She doesn't know anything about me. She has no reason to fear me. It's just a look I've always had. Yesterday Grand Uncle Peter observed that my countenance is that of someone who would laugh in the face of Satan himself given the chance. My grand uncle said, "You were an odd child, you were an odd woman, and now you're an odd old bat. Nothing's more dangerous than a female like that." The silver cross around the nurse's neck dangles from side to side. Every now and then she touches it, as if I'm a vampire who might leap up from this bed, pounce on her, and perhaps, unmoor her from her gradual, comfortable descent into death.

I wish I possessed that sort of power. I wish I was as dangerous as everyone seems to think I am. You know what I'd do? I'd go out and find Satan; I'd dig him up if I needed to, but wouldn't bother laughing in his face. Instead, I'd fasten him to a prayer—an anchor wrapped around his neck three times—and send him flying back so, so far. He'd never get the chance.

I'm 26 again.

I don't like 26.

26, I have a sister. 26, Satan drives up in a shiny convertible and coaxes her inside with his sweet promises. 26, Satan gets his dirty hands around her neck. 26, I had a sister.

I pray it different every day that follows.

"There you are," says Mama, tying the faded apron around her waist. "Your skin is looking dry. And these spots! Are you still using that crème I got you?"

"Is it so wrong, after all?" I ask her. "To pray out of order? Now that you've had time to think about it."

Her knees are tucked away beneath sensible trousers, and I can't help but miss the short, colorful dresses she used to wear. But, she's still Mama, despite the halving of her joy and proliferation of her sorrows. "I don't see," she says, "the sense in wasting your time talking with our Lord about what's already over and done."

"Is time so precious that I need to be so very sparing with it?"

"Child, you have no idea."

Mama's 42, she's 49, she's 67, she's 74. She looks backwards more with each year that passes. She concerns herself less with sacrilege. She grips my hand as she reclines in the hospital bed, or is it the other way around? "I'll race you," I wanted to say, but she wouldn't get the joke.

Today she prances into my room, making sure the nurse didn't leave anything in the wrong place. When the great aunts get talking too loud, she shushes them. When the breeze blows too cold on my bed, she closes the window. She's 25.

"Is Agnes with you?" I ask.

"That depends," Mama says, "on how hard you keep praying."

"Thought you said it was a waste of time."

"Might as well give it a shot—what else are you going to do lying there in that bed?"

There's always enough time, until finally there isn't. I'll use what I have left.

26, Satan, go to hell. 26, Satan, sleep in today. 26, Satan, forget where you left the keys. 26, Satan, get a head cold and stumble to the doctor's office begging for drugs. 26, Satan, eat a poisoned piece of pie, every delicious piece, and suffer until you die. 26, Satan, get in a bar fight you can't possibly win. 26, Satan, crawl into a deep, deep hole and stay put forever. 26, Satan, find the Lord if you must, but find him far, far from here.

26, Satan, see her standing on the side of the road—see her hopeful and young—and just keep driving.

Amen.

The nurse cracks the door back open and looks inside.

"Are we being too loud?" I ask.

"We?"

It's a "we" with all the most frightening ideas she can conjure nestled inside, because she hasn't done this job that long—hasn't gotten expert at the strange business of letting people go. She doesn't realize a room might look empty but not be. A few years from now, she'd be at my side, handing me empty comfort and pretending she hasn't read the signs. Instead she stares at my bed, eyes wide, fingers reaching for that silver cross. She's 40. Don't worry, 40. It hurts now, but every heartbreak can be unraveled. Every loss undone. Turns out, prayers travel in whichever direction we want.

I'm 27.

I have a sister.

—**Sarah Lofgren** (she/her)

Blood

Life takes shape between my legs,
a universe held in such a small space.
My breaths are labored, my body aches.
I bring a new soul into a brand new day.
His eyes meet mine, a storm at sea,
my eyes a whole canopy of trees.

Six months from now, I'll begin to bleed,
watch it drip down from my legs
that were the gateway to immortality
and plug it like it's an offensive sight
to cycle with a moon who sits amongst stars
while men gaze up at the sky in awe.

—**Cat Speranzini** (she/her)

The Author Gives the People What They Want

What if I poet-ed
all my trauma
in these little mini
morsels of words,

& then ended it
with something biting
so they have something
to sticker their
Stanley cups with?

Does it feel good? Do you like the scars I bleed out on here? Do you want it ephemeral?

Would you like
      the unknown
        the unknown
          the u n k n o w n

SOMEthing B R O
            ken   &&&   BEAU tiful.

            The people keep mouthing but not making sounds "wow!!! he really plays with
                                    F O RM!!!!!"

WILL YOU LOVE ME NOW ??? WILL YOU TAKE THE REJECTION LETTERS & UNBLEED ALL THE
PAPERWOUNDS YOU MADE ME BLEED ???
      I
            AM
                  UNBOTHERED

I swear
I swear
 I swear I'm not petty & I'm not
      PANDERING

            I swear I'm not made for this, it's all just nightmare head hunting ...
                        it's all just the games we play with each other.

&&& when I'm hungry
I lick the plate clean & I do not ask for more.

One hand is always somewhere near my throat & the other
is reaching for my heart.

It seems like all I do these days is lament
which is usually a sexy thing to do
but my candle burns inward
so now everyone is concerned instead of turned on.

I wish I could tell you   that the weight of how I treat myself
has actually taken its toll   but I think I can still keep kicking
myself while I'm down.

AMAZING ISN'T IT ??? How much the body
can withstand before becoming something

u n r e c o g n i z a b l e.

—**Gabriel Noel** (he/him)

Live to let lie
   —*in memory of N. Popenko*

Wrinkled eyes on a sleepless night
pouch the blue with blurred red corners.
They blink sharply on and spin swiftly closed.
(Oh, the things I wish you knew.)

She said the light would find my way
but it came too soon and left me wondering,
What lay beyond the midnight corner
with winds that danced on moonlit floors?

"Just sing our song," she faintly sighed
with lips that catered to velvet strings.
"We'll own the night, we'll run too far
on paths that turn on hips and sprains."

But I knew too much and you too few
of pages wrapped in shadows and gold.
We'd twist and swim 'till sunset ends
with starfish dressed in Triton's ore.

I live to let lie, what's done is gone—
her silhouette runs free on canvas walls.
An iris core hides still, undiscovered.
Wrinkled eyes on a sleepless night.

—**Carly Popenko** (she/her)

Untitled – Maya Collins (she/her)

SWALLOW

i think
i swallowed an(other?) person.

slurped her down
with that bottle-and-a-half
of / *fizz whizz pop!* / champagne

or maybe

she slipped into my lips
parted in swelling moons
while i slept

slinked down down
my spine
breathed hot air
on my pussy
o!

but really
it probably happened
when i fucked my professor's wife.

—she's started finger
knitting in my brain
teasing all the wrinkles
& folds apart into skeins

i don't recognize her voice
even though it is my
tongue my teeth

blue dogs bark bark wildly back!

—**Nora Boyle** (she/her)

Dinosaurs and IVF or Being Queer and Having Kids in the Apocalypse

In two organs the size of a walnut, I have 200,000 eggs. They have lived inside me for longer than I have lived, since I was, according to the internet, the size of a grapefruit, a banana, a troll doll. Then, at 20 weeks old, there were 7 million of them, a New York City's worth of half-me's, midtown and skyscrapers and crisscrossed bridges, commutes and matinee's of me's, snowy-window Christmas dinners of me's, a tableful of me's at Sardi's, waiting for the review of my new play, written by my worst critic—me. It is this image that flashes through my mind the first time you make a joke about how much sunscreen our kids will need, the laughter, and then the realization. That our children will be ours, ours, but not made of the two of us. A New York City's worth of me's pressing their faces to the glass, seeing only a reflection. A city of faces looking out and seeing nothing.

20

weeks. When I was halfway through becoming a being that could breathe air and open my eyes, I carried already these 7 million possibilities, floating in the natal darkness of a woman in a small wintery town. For twenty weeks, it was all of us in there, considering whatever was to be considered then. Once, I was one of 7 million possibilities my mother held, as my grandmother held her. And so it goes, back and back, and in this way, we have all known countries we never set foot in, lived fights we didn't flinch from, dreamed, inside a dream, inside a dream.

160

million years ago, the dream begins, just as Pangea begins to drift apart. It begins in Jurassic-era China, with a shrew named Juramaia. At just under three inches long, the average size of a man's thumb, or the size of a bumblebee hummingbird, Juramaia is the first mammal to give birth. She does this alone, in a burrow, without knowing what will happen to her.

65

million years ago, the Maiasaura lives in what is now called Montana. She is an elegant dinosaur with a long, sloping neck, a broad mouth, often greened and pollen dusted from grazing on wildflowers, and wet, soulful eyes. This is an embellishment on my part—we cannot actually know what the dinosaur's eyes looked like. But Maiasaur was a plant eater, a herd animal, the aunty-in-spirit of the cow, the deer, the manatee. I don't need a fossil record to know she had kind eyes.

185

million years ago, a mother is in Arizona. She is Kayentatherium, a thing between many things. A mammal-like reptile, or reptile-like mammal. Semi-aquatic. Semi-mammalian. We know that she loved to swim. To climb the arches. Maybe to look at the sky. I tell myself I know her, because I, too, live here and love those things. When we find her, 185 million years later, it is from her footprints. Too deep in the mud, trying desperately to escape a rising river. To deep, for her bodyweight. Too deep, we know, once we find the body, because she died carrying her 38 babies on her back. I realize I don't know her at all. I don't know if I could carry that much.

5

years ago, we have the first conversation about children. It is mostly a catalogue of maybes. Maybe we want them, maybe we don't. Maybe we couldn't afford them. Maybe we could. Maybe we want to stay forever this way, coming and going as we please. Maybe it would ruin everything.

4

years ago, we wonder. What if there was a way. What if you carried them. What if I did. What if we saved. What if we couldn't save them from what was coming.

65

million years ago, Maiasaura is living in a green valley, near what will someday be called Choteau, Montana. She has never seen a human being, and we will never see her, because one day (before there are days of the week, or even months, when the sun and its turning really is the only calendar), one day, an asteroid the size of Mount Everest will careen into the Yucatán Peninsula going 100,000 kilometers per hour, releasing a detonating force equivalent to 10 billion atomic bombs.

2020

When we talk about children—over breakfast eaten on the floor, watching nature documentaries, in the car on the way to wait, masked, in the parking lot of a grocery store, in bed, in the dark, in the silences between passing cars, what we come back to is this: how can we bring them into this world?

This world in which I call myself an environmentalist. I'm a vegan. I take the bus. I recycle. But there's still a part of me, the part of me nestled close to my granny's granny's granny, that looks at you and wants to know what your eyes would look like, gazing up from a little potential. Our maybe. A baby who is already contained in me, or you, but who cannot be in both of us. And yet, a baby that is still possible, the doctors say. The strangeness of it all, to be the first of our kind. A new plotpoint on the evolutionary tree. Our generation, the first to be able to dream of this glass-creation. Our eggs in a nest of reflection, our me's staring out the window, our faces pressed against the glass. Unimaginable to the past. One hundred years ago, or fifty years ago, or twenty years ago, it would not be possible, what we are considering. The choice we have available. And there is no question: for us, it is a choice. We are not afforded the luxury of an accident.

667

trees. Per person. Per year. 667 trees breathing away on a mountaintop somewhere, to drink in the effects of our life. Our trips to the movies. Our avocados. Our doctor's appointments.

What do I say to that. What is a maybe worth. What are 667 trees worth. What am I paying with. How far do I sit from the end of the dream.

How long until the fire goes out.

∞

time. Mythic time. Time not as a line, but as a fabric, your sweatshirt bundled up and tossed in the corner. As liquid, the teacup at your bedside. As present, as in gift, as in I am bumping into you the night we met, I am sleeping, always on the left, I am walking down the aisle again, and again, and I am in kindergarten saying I don't know what I want to be when I grow up yet, but that I still have time. As cycle, you bleeding then me, me bleeding then you. As spiral, the pattern on the belly of the tadpoles I saved from puddles when I was still close enough to my mother to remember darkness. Time as again, and again, and again. Am I willing to be an ending.

In mythic time, I am already being eaten. I have crawled into the nest of a grave, I am smiling to the earthy stars with a mossy tombstone of herbivore teeth as worms learn the crests of my body. I am at peace, finally, already, just glad to be of use. To stop consuming. The worms learn, as you once did.

In mythic time, the ghost of Maiasaura is in my t-shirt. It makes sense that we are all made of each other. I drive to a doctor's appointment, the engine a swarm of plankton and the deep places of the earth, fire.

In mythic time, my question is no question. There is just the stretch in all directions, an unbroken line, not straight, but stitching, bringing me together again and again with all my thanksgivings, giving thanks to Juramaia, to Westlothiana, to Icthyostega and Agnatha and Cyanobacteria. Thank you for lungs, I say as the asteroid looms. Thank you for teeth. For hips. For blood, for bleeding. For sight and all the things we see. Thank you, living breathing endless pieces that brought me to this maybe. The world is burning.

43

nests. In a valley in Montana, there are 43 nests.

We know about the Maiasaura, because of the picture they left us. The Pompeian lovers. The moment of impact.

43 nests, raised berms of earth in perfect circles. Inside them, eggs. Delicate. Unbroken. Eggs, complete with translucent, unfinished bones inside, even though

65

million years ago, a stone breaks the silence. Craters the earth. It is heard around the world, flash of light, wall of water, rock-strewn sky. A curtain of fire crosses the continent faster than a fighter jet, arrives, less than an hour later, at the Maiasaura and her nest.

43

Maiasaura climb atop the small craters, the berms, their worlds. They lay down, smooth bellies to the earth. Above, stones re-enter the atmosphere at speed faster than the fastest bullet we have created, it begin to rain fire. But to the little ones, with the cool, familiar bulk of their mothers between them and the world, the known darkness of the nest, the pattering of this fiery rain thrumming through the earth, to them, it feels different than a summer thunderstorm. Seems, for the longest time, as though it will pass.

2023

We have already chosen names, though I don't know if we will use them.

65

million years later, a Paleontologist finds them, hundreds of them, the first dinosaur eggs to have survived the weight of the world ending, time and time again. They debate genus, species, phylum, and in the end, a name is chosen.

They name her Maiasaura. The good mother.

—**Ro Smith** (they/them)

First published by ISLE: Interdisciplinary Studies in Literature and Environment

The Women Don't Burn, They Fly

"mad sensuality corrupted her so"
—Dante's Inferno

had there been fruit on the trees
we would have eaten it up by dawn

we lived like the red fox, the cottontail
in our own little pocket of night

and don't you think I'd scoop
all of our tiny bodies out of that year

cup my hand gently and bring us to the air
like precious metal panned from a stream

stamp away the want in those
little fucking boys

a whole goddamn infestation
come to feast on us girls—

girls placed on the front lines with empty hands
learning to make wounds of our bodies

while mother licked a finger to wipe at us
like a smudge, cursed our budding breasts

then picked up her own small box of prayer,
I'd rather scales to shed than this female fur

mothers please tell me—what did you want from us.
teaching silence & expecting song

when the whole world was the other side
of a closed door on Saturday night

and on Sunday I'm somewhere
between the house of the devil

and a holy space that taught me
to unearth all my brokenness

still, know that I prayed with my eyes open
but if you asked me now I would say

there's no god in that town—just the mothers
arms outstretched their voices

like a hymn that's bitter on the tongue
& there wasn't a one of us that made it out

not against slick hands under skirts
midnight fists knocking or open windows

girls that once curled in bed like cats
our softness confounding

before the boys found us—
they spoke sweetness in darkened rooms

lips peeled back, bodies ripe with whiskey
holding some kind of secret

we were told we wanted
the whole world screaming us into

small pretty things, tiny gifts
stacked up neatly as nesting dolls

and we dropped from the sky
we cracked, we caved, we fell

laid out like carrion
the town picked us clean

so drive us from your doors
clip our wings cut out our hearts

confine us to a storm
pack us in like starlings

we fly with the wind of a thousand
women, knees raw with prayer

to a god that never came
to a man that would never come

bring us to the pyre for opening our legs
strike a match because we thought it was love

—**Lauren Kalstad** (she/her)

Night wanderings

chest throbbing
claustrophobic, she rises
crosses the threshold
of bamboo bungalow
like a barefoot bird

hair like black mambas
entangled in tree refuge
the town asleep except
for curious hawkers, their eyes
glowing in the dark

volcanoes roar
villagers dream of twin souls
shadow of a small brown cat
accompanying, distant thunder
screams in the moonlight

she arrives at a river
feet damp from the
night soil,
ghost footprints
tending to fields of rice

immersing into water
white nightgown clinging
like a wide-eyed tarsier
a sharp rock pierces
her foot

she wakes—gasping, trembling
reaches for damp riverbank
surrendering her eyelashes
to seedlings planted in mud
the earth shudders at her touch

on this side of the river
her warm crossing body
will only be known
as *babaylan,*
the healer

—**Rina Malagayo Alluri** (she/her)

Three Sisters – Patricia Feinman (she/her)

Venus of Willendorf

I desperately call to Venus
in my time of need. Blood leaks
from between my limp legs.
My tears cool my hot cheeks.

I've betrayed you by returning
the gift you gave me.
But to me it was no gift,
it was unwanted, unexpected.
I've saved it from this wretched earth.
Baptized in blood it returns
to you cradled in white.
Forgive me Venus.

She appears to me in her soft orange ochre
Her bowed head of plaits shakes
at me and her hands, glued to her chest,
hover over her beating heart.
I hear the soft thumps against her ribs
and the rhythm calms me.

Child, I will not punish you
for you have chosen a selfless act
in your decision to save it.

Her blessing rains over me
in a cool hospital breeze.
She disappears in the flutter
of the curtain. I lift the covers
greeted by a puddle of blood
a reminder of my sacrifice.

—**Azaliyah Molina** (she/they)

A Toast to All Our Hells

There's little mystery left to men in this day and age. From factory workers to salarymen, they sit either in assembly lines or tinker in dinky offices, thirsting after long forgotten days of carnage, war, and glory in video games and Gloria Et Romana. The grey ghosts of this world bury their masculine Ids six feet under, where my husband Samael lives.

There isn't much left in this world to intrigue an ancient goddess. Lilith, they call me, killer of infant souls. Queen of Hell, Nightmare Raven, Seed-Stealer and Seductress. Yet men have their little kinks I find intriguing, tiny cracks in the modern Ubermensch that display the inner animal—and women, beneath their painted cheeks and milquetoast vanilla note perfumes, can be even more vicious and unhinged.

Oh, how I love the sons of Adam and daughters of Eve. I was there when Rome burned, fiddling Nero off in his marble bathtub. I came to Joan of Arc in her prison, promised her a happy place in my military after *dear* old Michael had abandoned his protégé to the stake. I picked Jezebel's remains from dogs' teeth and gave her a proper burial, wept with Bathsheba and raged with her the night her husband was killed and David raped her—bastards always, those unfallen Sons of God.

I mourned with the Marys. I am the Shekinah's handmaiden, after all, and I serve Sophia in my own ways— *Iesu* was her most loved child. All I am is an afterthought, a cautionary fable turned feminist icon. I plotted with my old lover Chava to liberate our daughters, and we poked Marie Curie and Margaret Sanger enough to invent modern science and birth control, worked up the Brontës and Austen into inventing the Gothic and romance novel, inspired Rosa not to give up her seat (but thanks, dear, for the poisoned offer), and above all—*we raged*. Chava and I raged. We still rage.

It's been a long day. Countless women and children murdered. Samael brings home the dead, laboring always in reverse birth pangs as the Reaper, and Eve and I tend their souls, helping them pass on with the aid of Gabriel, Lailah, and Dumah. I needed a break. I needed a bar.

So here I am, New York City on Christmas Eve, a Jewish girl with no reason to celebrate (Samael has spoiled me at Hanukah), and I am in a little black slip of nothing and faux minx fur muff (murdering animals is something I could never do. Children either, for the matter—the older rabbis always got my story wrong. Mine was a story of what women were *owed*, not what we *stole*), with a Tisch ballerina at my side. Her name is Raquel.

We share drinks. Toast the night. Kiss—her lips are like cherries—and I take her back to my palatial penthouse that towers in a razor-thin metal needle above Central Park. I lay Raquel down on a bed of black silk and white roses, and with my tongue, sex, and fingers, I spoil my little dancer rotten.

The church bells toll for Christmas. The arrival of a Savior I care not a whit for—I still wait for some fabled Messiah to come. Then, the Shekinah can ascend, freed from her perpetual sleep, and I and my sisters Agrath, Eisheth, and Naamah will be made into the Horae again, and Samael shall lose the poisonous Mem from his name—*Samael turned to Sa'el*—and become one of Heaven's most shining covenants.

For now, I smoke a Virginia Slim as snow falls over the Hudson. Raquel is lounging in bed, drinking hot cocoa. Her blonde hair reminds me of my lover Chava. But her breasts are too tiny and pearled to bear the First Mother's burden. I am the Last Mother, Birther of Monsters (though Chava labored with many of Samael's own in her exile from Adam, and now Adam prefers the gold stones of sterile Heaven to any rich roses of Hell), and I?

I am left to carry on, picking girls piece by piece up after honor killings, wiping away tears after acid attacks, mending wombs and baby bones back together after back-alley abortions forced upon minors by beer-stinking uncles and cousins.

Chava and I ride the North Wind.

We bring in the forgotten.

We still champion freedom.

And we remember the women.

All of them.

Raquel sighs lightly in her sleep, and I tuck her gently in, kiss her brow, and smile at this daughter of Lilith, this daughter of Eve—so tender are our daughters in their passions, so kind and loving in their gaze.

It makes a woman proud to be a mother.

I ride the Black Horse, Eve champions the White Mare.

She brings in the Living, I bring in the Dead.

Womb and Tomb, the Oak and Ivy, Forever

And Ever

Entwined.

—**Allister Nelson** (she/her)

Signature

Rosebuds blossom next to Christ's ~~Crux~~ Gammadion—
flowers: Chrysanthemums, jasmine, lotuses...
tantric reverse swastikas with angels' wings,
grim reaper scythes, and inverted pentagrams.
Demons pluck the petals in the summer heat, ah.

I draw there in the dirt and diesel a rose bud;
my predetermined sexuality will lay plain
for all to see, but a verbally abusive patriot
will rebuke my pride, and I will be caused to repress
my sexuality until I can thoroughly emasculate myself.

I am a starry-eyed child in a dark classroom, *blink*—
I am the scrawl teenager taking shape, *blink*—
I am an acoustic mind in the cyberstream, *blink*—
I am smeared grease, an obfuscated expression.

X marks the spot next to "name:_____"
Except a new alias has bloomed along the line.

—**Xavier Zane Wherley** (they/them)

gutter maps

ocean ellipsis mouth
we catch ourselves
a grumble in the time gap
maw's energetic swallow
her beast, her quickening

where were all the murderous
bowlegged dangers i avoided
roller-skating down Mermaid Avenue
back when tides washed the back legs of youth's agency

there in the subatomic catacomb
an organism of prisms
sold in the back junk shops

i washed my poverty in anonymous
erotic paperbacks i washed
my ideas about poverty through
the camera's ground glass

the smiling was a circle
i swung to—the sun
beat the boardwalk and its

nostalgic catastrophe of magics
a map of gaslight gutter
rainbows i followed to the sea

—Melissa Eleftherion (she/they)

you see me

When I look at myself, I like to block off my chest with the edge of the mirror or my arms and hands. Sometimes I spread them apart and down allowing my gaze to softly focus on the skin just below the collarbone—my brain fills in the rest—*they're just pecs.* I fantasize about wearing buttonless vests, naked underneath, sun painting my glistening skin. I tape my chest and feel free until the itching begins as the adhesive wears on my skin. I wanna wear a thin white tank-top without any fear of my tits taking up more space than my face, my voice. I've stopped buying bras, even though I need them—I just wanna throw them all away. When he avoided my breasts aside from light nipple play I felt like myself and I want that feeling to be effortless—that *I woke up like this* energy—brushing my teeth in my boxers, topless. I just want to keep them guessing as I spiral into myself—maybe splatter. I wanna know a lover wants me for me and not the body I embody involuntarily. I wanna wear a tight shirt, a halter top, a bandeau, maybe even a skirt— without any tremor of doubt that you'll know, I am who I am as I am. That I'll be perceived correctly: *boy.*

People who don't know me almost always refer to me as she, but the first thing you ever said to me was, *boy, you a sparkle.* Some folks can't get past my tits but you wanna get on your knees to suck me. *I wanna drink your cum, dude.* You make me feel like a real boy with all these—bruh - bro - guy - dude - boy - daddy - dean's. Baby boy, baby boy, you compliment my mind—my nature—and my ass.

I arrive: you kiss my neck, my cheek, my neck, my mouth—I greet the wall with my back and your tongue with force. You have a magic mouth and make your bed in the morning. Chai tea—*this is an uptown spliff*— earth on my tastebuds. You have a blue guitar, it's almost as beautiful as you. You might be the prettiest boy I've ever kissed. I wanna shake you like a baby or something—wear you like a backpack, I don't know. All you do is smile when you look at me. You rest your hand on my thigh, right above the knee, just under my pant leg—your hand is warm, soft. You're a soft 'n' fiery boy: a ram. *Beautiful, sir*—slap me or something—*let me grab a condom*—my clit adores you. I wonder how long that'll last. I watch your mouth all shiny with my cum while you tell me stories. *Talk to me endlessly, daddy.*

When we kissed before falling asleep, I felt all kinds of things in my chest. I didn't wanna feel so sweet 'bout you, but our feet were tangled 'n' soft together, our feet all heavy. You kissed me tender as if I were the sand on the beach and you the current, lapping me up. A sunset of orange and green flooded my eyelids. We held each other sleeping despite our preference not to. *I'm cuddly but I like my personal space.* That tender shit really pulls at my heart, 'n' all the pheromones, ya know? I woke up to the rain and the sun and your face at ease.

Morning, sir. You eat a waffle out the toaster full of wheat 'n' try to kiss me—*wash your mouth first.* You smile 'n' wash out the crumbs. I kiss you; peppermint. You walk me to your door 'n' kiss me again, grabbing me. *Let me know you make it home safe, boy.*

—**Dean Jones** (he/they)

altared

bring me flowers
rootless, bright
smiling

I will declare them
as offerings at
my altar

kiss them
as they
wilt

keep them
even after
they begin to droop

I would frame them
lay them in my heart's
corner
shining on its infinite walls

beauty does last
in the intentions
of small things

like how you grab
my wrists
turn them up to
graze soft lips
on melting skin

as I am ice
upon your touch
I burn into water

or how you caress
my feet so that
even on the most
tired of days

my soles bloom
into lotus flowers

anything given by your hands
would be a treasure
I would keep till
I too wilt

with the hopes that
you will come and kiss me

mount me in your heart
as I blossom in death
on your infinite walls.

—ena ganguly (she/they)

& They Called Us Venus Flytraps – Alé Cota (they/she)

"Unless one lives and loves in the trenches, it is difficult to remember that the
\war against dehumanization is ceaseless." —Audre Lorde, *Sister Outsider*

sZZZZz
        hotly dripping
        solar stares startle   this starred stray   sitting on cement.
i collect debt debated from skinned smiles   (the price of no home)
i'm stared as if this loss illegible   (girl, boy, object)
        as if this body   unreachable   (no salvation)
c'mon jimmy don't look undeniably   (i'm in my best dress)
the blond bear bewares her babies from me   since then i
                abandon respectability

toco toco toco toco   i spin with the surveilling bird eye above
i've sowed streets   like a frenzied fiend
once i saw this woman   (& only have seen women)
        she lingered in the same spot
        wore a cape backward   an angel's bib
        its edges   charred feather tips
        whipped like pistons   locomotive to eat
        debri-dandelions   i'm sure it was delicious
            in dreams we kiss & make love
i join our temple tents   our sanctuary   she holds me
& i whisper   flowery blessings into her & rub nectar on her lips
just in case   it seals us like honey.   & i wake up.
               her name was Morning.

WHACK! i slam gym locker #39   my closet
is wrapped in my sister's hand-me-down towel
i splish-sploosh under the crystalline shower head
she's goooorge   i think   lathering my fingers skate across my
soaped foliage   i miss   touch   on this
oiled page   i miss   being dog-eared alive
flesh folds of love i mistook   this   concaving for
The Second Coming   but feminine bodies   don't receive second grace
my steamed mirror shy   the handle inside me thumping.
turns out   fleeing family   frees you slightly nonetheless i flew
& landed into a tight-lipped lie: rock-bottom
can still be a bed   this fogged corner taught me
freedom is the fly endlessly feeding
                  Venus.

How Many Women

how many women
read the whole thing
and fall in love

I know better

I pour another glass
and toast an English muffin

—**L. Lois** (she/her)

The Sky, Now Blue

The grains of sand cradle your feet, filling the spaces between your toes and hugging the backs of your heels. The brininess, the certain density that the salt gives to the wet air soothes your uneasy head. It's playing tricks with you again.

The beach is her favorite place. You know that because she told you when you started walking along the shoreline. She loves how the ocean breeze waltzes with her long hair. She loves the asymmetry of opalescent seashells, the ruffled feathers of the gulls, and the crystalline waves. You watch her pick up a vine of kelp and squeeze the bulbs between her fingers, delighting with every pop.

You can't remember the last time you'd eaten. You pat your stomach, feeling the sweater and the waistband of your jeans—those you remember putting on, what? Yesterday? Two days ago?

The late afternoon sun casts an ethereal glow around her while the wind paints strokes of deep pink on her cheeks and blows strands of her free-flowing hair across her face. As you watch the reflection of crashing waves through her eyes, you notice that each blink, each flutter of her eyelashes initiates a new sparkling rush of the water. You surrender to the refuge.

The coast stretches for miles; you'll turn back soon. To your right, the uninterrupted Pacific. To your left, a tall sand dune speckled with ice plants and zips of digger bees. You can't see over the edge.

"Isn't it nice here?" She collects your attention from the dune's peak. You smile, nodding.

You come to an area where the sand is more hard-packed than usual. You can barely see your own footprints and hers aren't visible at all. You watch sand crab holes bubble with each ebbing tide while the languid ocean hums and rolls.

The sky looks like an oil spill. Not dark and leaky; the pretty part where green and magenta swirl around each other.

Maybe an oil spill isn't the right thing to call it.

"Like the outside of a bubble," she says. Once again, you nod in agreement.

She walks ahead of you. An overwhelming urge to embrace her lurches your arm forward. You reach for her hand, but your efforts are as successful as trying to grasp a ray of light. She is too enthralled with the blanched skeleton of a sand dollar to notice. A breeze whips your hair into your eyes, over your cheekbones, and across the nape of your neck.

You frown, running your fingers through chin-length hair. You haven't worn it that long in years. You examine your hands, hovering with a noticeable shake. The cuticle edge of your chipped pink nail polish sits nearly halfway up your nailbed. The tips of her toes and the hem of her billowing dress enter your vision.

"How long have I been here?" you ask.

Her smiling face, held uncomfortably close to yours, dulls. You've seen this look before in your dreams when you ask someone for the date or the time.

"How long have I been here?" you repeat yourself. Her eyes are wincing with confusion, maybe even betrayal.

"How   long?"

"Yes—"

"   Ha ve yo u?"

"How long have I—"

"b   e en ?"

"h   e r   e?   "

Your body tenses at her malfunction.

"It   sh   o   uld

ha   v   e b   ee   n

y   ou."

You watch as her face begins to collapse into itself the way wet sand crumbles under its own weight, the way two conflicting swells make a cross sea. Her nose folds into the right corner of her mouth and you can see what deciduous teeth she has left fanning and unfurling across her cheek, pushed out by their permanent replacements. Her eyes go wide at first—so wide that the full, dark circles of her irises are visible as the color spills out of them, fading away like ink left in the sun. She squeezes them shut, eyelids buckling under the weight of her furrowed brow.

"H ow   lon g?   "

Chills scrape up your spine and over your shoulders while each of her lashes crosses into its opposing lid and digs itself under her tender skin, stitching and pulling them shut. You can see the dislocation of her lower jaw, gapping, twisting, tearing under the flesh, and her pale, chapped tongue struggling to form the sounds—cutting itself on the fine line between echolalia and understanding.

"   How l   ong   ha ve   I   be en her e   ?"

Her broken voice shatters your fragile sanctuary and suspends your heart above a depth destined for implosion. Your stomach churns, face burning with a roaring sadness. Your throat cracks from the screams she should be hearing, but the wind carries the sound away before it can reach her.

Together, you throw your heads back to the sky, sending silent wails from heaving chests. The tendons running across your neck and through your arms stretch and hyperextend, as if trying to climb out from under layers of dermal tissue. A thud of her knees at your feet, arms wrapped tight around your waist, blurring face pushing into your stomach—you can't look down at her, even when she gnaws and chews at your flesh. You cradle her head in one hand, the other pushes at her shoulder.

Your burning eyes catch a glimpse of the sky, now blue.

You can see the blotchiness of the white clouds and where the cerulean paint didn't quite settle into the commercial ceiling tile. The fluorescent lights on either side of the painted panel hummed in an otherwise quiet and colorless room.

How long have you been here?

You sit up and a cacophony of sound breaks the stillness as your hospital gown moves against the crinkled table paper beneath you. Your sweater and jeans wait folded on the chair in the corner.

—**Jordan Nishkian** (she/her)

Medusa

let's play double-dutch with our tongues
tie them into pretty bows
then slip them into the backs of our throats
for safekeeping

so many men have snatched, gobbled
up my words, left me tongue-tied
called it romantic, told me
"i know you like that"

i want a tongue with venom
& a skin that sheds
want lovers to bow down
feel my Medusa mouth snake
over their skin

i want kisses that blind
lips painted red, like spilled blood
i'll spill blood
i'll spill your blood
if i have to

but right now
i want to kiss you
like we're playing jump rope
with bubblegum mouths & sugar on our lips
but i won't let you take anymore
of my words or
my stories

i'll fasten my tongue into a noose
if i have to,

darling.

—**Nora Boyle** (she/her)

Shakti

On nights like this I turn into myself, cosmic yonic
to the bud, a dome egg, lurid eight-armed principality. My
body a beckoned universe, light amber gold, my arms
the dent of runes scored onto great
      stone. Reflective mirror water. My
eyes an ancient world beget in ruin, an all-seeing all-loving
Angel. The bath I draw
is filled with white jasmine, soft feminine
righteousness, my bed a basket of offerings
left uneaten. Sleepless. My emotions a scarlet roil beneath
my feet. Perpetually enlightened
and awake, my own divine awareness. My
hair melts like wax paper. It is holy in
the way people faint before their god, the way
believers tremble before they fall, walk a thousand
      miles barefoot on hot sand. I have to move in order
to touch the post of my bed. My
pillows plush deities decked out in lush fabric, running
through my fingers like a river. Fever. I am at one with My
self, I am sure of it. The curtains are loved by
my hands, gauzy brahmin, this sickness but
a facet of my power. I consult and consort
      the rain-filled sky, pray to it, court it like how Shiva
courted Sati. My bedroom perfectly ephemeral, soundless
and soulful, the female form a masterpiece of being.

—**Cheryl Tan** (she/her)

Untitled – Irina Tall (Novikova) (she/her)

Rice and Eggs

Melt butter in a pan

Back pressed against the chilling brown tile, knees slightly bent to fit, wet hair pricking against eyelids, mouth open to gnaw at the jet assaulting the face, streams spill down the body; tracing a line from the raised white bumps on the chin, to the yellowed, shrinking breast tissue, to the violet rib indentations, to the already blisteringly scarlet itching legs, where they fall off to circle the drain before disappearing from view.

Boil salted water

Cold concrete beneath soaked feet leads dust to instantly attach itself to the soles before there is an opportunity for socks. One hand desperately clutches hotel travel shampoo, the other grasps at the permanently dampened towel. Shivers escape the dark blue cloth, leading to it being tightened around the chest, binding the form until it is restrained flat but finally comfortably lukewarm. A single drop falls from the black hair into the mouth which purses in consideration. Momentary hesitation replaced by the towel moving to dry the perpetrating hair like a flat iron.

Scramble one egg

The towel threatens to wiggle free from the hip prison it is currently tied to. An orange cylindric container is grasped by the hand. The equally nauseatingly orange lid rests on the speckled marble counter. The nozzle cap pops off against the pressure of the thumb, dangling from the nozzle by the plastic string binding the two together. White lotion squirts directly onto the planned, dry left shoulder, the right wrist is moved to remove evidence of the deed done by rubbing circularly, the wrist vein is smothered in testosterone before being wiped off against newly acquired dark, curled, lower stomach hairs.

Add rice, stirring clockwise

Pale, strained hands grasp at the lifeline bathroom counter as eyes focus around the dark grey spots gradually spiraling outward, its webs overtaking vision for a moment. The eyes shut when vision is completely lost, allowing them to relax. A breath travels from the brain frantically repeating the counts of "4,7,8" to the nose which shoves them down into the throat where the lungs greedily grasp at it, holding it hostage until the mouth remembers to remove it from the premises. This cycle repeats, painfully not automated, until the eyes slowly peel open and are rewarded with fully saturated vision. Nausea climbs the up ladder from the empty expanse of the stomach before getting stuck in the scratched-up throat where it pops against the larynx and disperses.

Remove from heat

Too big underwear is shoved up past both legs with the hopes that it will stay in place, despite the absence of once supporting hips. The comb is a constant force, traveling down from the indented scalp to the fraying ends that have already started to curl contrarily. Palms rub chai scented CBD oil over sore spots before tucking the chest into the faded gray sports bra deemed tolerable. The comb somehow still strains water droplets which fall primarily on the striped socks that read "Pretty Decent Boyfriend". They seem to seek the socks out with a mission to make an already uncomfortable sensory experience entirely unbearable. Alongside the rasping of the treading-water comb, the right shoulder extends outward with a pop, creating rubber-band-like tension, waiting for it to snap back into its assigned place. The purple cotton shirt travels down the arms, clinging to the still moistened flesh masses.

Let sit with steam until fully cooked

Red "easy open arthritis" cap in one hand, two baby blue ovals in the other. Removal of two silver rings from the index finger which then pushes the ovals past the sandpaper-esque tongue into the back of the throat. The pills are held in uvula limbo, slowly sinking into the pink throat as the hand grasps the black metal water bottle adorned with stickers, swallowing the few drops left inside and sending the pills rushing down to their job of temporary relief.

Serve with soy sauce

The body claims most of the stained, off-white couch. Legs tuck under each other, weaving into a numbing mess of limbs. A black charging cable snakes from the laptop resting on the ottoman, onto the left knee, up past the shoulder, to the white outlet underneath the decorative set of ribs of indeterminate origins used as a wall hanging. A turquoise plastic bowl drops onto the robe-covered lap. A mug of steaming specialty watery apple cinnamon tea is gently placed on the white wooden ends of the couch, resting there until needed. A rusting silver fork, pale yellow egg mass dotted with black pepper spots, white rice gradually sinking into the viscous brown liquid; a breakfast easy enough to force the stomach to accept.

—**Elwyn V.J Roth** (they/them)

#FFB3C6

The flush on my cheeks isn't a secret
Anymore, and the way the three p.m.
Sunset hits me every year is a call
Back to the version of me with
Stars in her eyes.

I am tearing myself out of here with all of
My body weight, none of anything about
What you see as I look up at you is an
Accident.
I didn't ask to be easy to figure out, and
I'm spitting cinnamon and venom at
The suggestion. I can't imagine a
Version of myself anyone's scared of,
Swore I didn't have the kind
Of anxiety that makes you mean, but
The tiny dog in me snips, and I don't mean
To, but I draw blood of my own type.

—Romy Rhoads Ewing (she/they)

(Wide) Awake

faces,   upside down in an aquarium of empty sockets in the ceiling fan a
flammable family   familiar   yet   no one has the same eyes or
or even goes to church   yet   we scratch at the same veins

just tonight in the shower my toenails sort of pile up in the drain   my skin
withers   like corn husks   my ears sprout cherry stems   i know how
onions feel   bleeding out on a cutting board

i used to be tan   now my face is a tributary of drunk elephant lala anti-wrinkle
cream   senescence chews on the crotch of my bagged-out panties
black thread unravels   like a primordial tampon string

              my body oozes   whenever   wherever it wants

the stains on the sheets aren't so bad   it's the rust on the mattress pad that
gets me   maybe I should buy a plastic liner?   ramp up the kegels?

instantly,   another light bulb bursts   an ejaculation of glass seeds with
microscopic tails   it's like trying to sleep under a colossal wishbone it's like

          what's the word?   where do they go?   words?

      thrashing in a bra with straps like raw lasagna noodles   it's stupid buying 4
oranges when only 3 fit in the bowl even when i'm in a bar i think of a mimosa
as a tree

startled by daylight   relatives sow roots in my pillow case   i play
with the lint in my pocket ball it up like a prayer bead and close my eyes
              subject of a new story

          of course i'm barefoot i'm in bed

—**Sherry Shahan** (she/her)

Untitled – Maya Collins (she/her)

blood dramatics

& it's all like yada
yada yada, the tomb looks
like a tomb &

> we've got blood for a few
> days. the human body can ex
> -sanguinate enough to die in as few

as five minutes. vampiric to the
touch, we sleep to
-gether enough to be clinically

> bedridden. your grandmother from
> Oklahoma writes on your Face
> -book how your entire family is

dying & can't afford to die so if you could
please find money in your heart. &
blood & sugar & loons in your

> eyes drain like pint
> glasses. we don't have to say it
> like we're fuck

-ing but (okay) we're (kind
of) fucking. she won't die or
she will. it's blood

> -letting, it's clarity without a bottle worth
> breaking. it's a tomb we don't love
> enough or can't build from

scratch. the heart is supposed to break.
it's made for entry &
exit. but where we rest,

> where we want to be for
> -ever. it can never be where
> we want it to be.

—**Liam Strong** (they/them)

My Childhood Hero Gives Me Panic Attacks – Maggie Bowyer (they/he)

My heroes
die.
The illusionist
perishes
Chords drift
toward me.

I find myself
<wrapped in baby blue sheets>   >shaking<   <his fists gripping me>

My fingers leave   sweat globs on the screen.   I try to delete   every memory

<remove song from playlist>

My vision doubles
>>>   trying   <<<   impressions   >>>

I am in two places at once and I am nowhere.

I AM EVERYWHERE BUT
I QUESTION MY EXISTENCE AT EACH JUNCTION.

the smell of death is a constant reminder
I am lurching toward the grave.
art is supposed to be a lifeline.
this has sucker-punched me
in a room with low oxygen.

My heroes die and I could be considered alive   >   i am starving and I wish someone would gently feed
me   /   not lies   /   nourish me   i am desperate for fodder   /   inspiration   /
representation   to touch the constellations marvel   at how my hands glimmer   refuse to triple check
if the universe withered

I AM BOTH ESSENTIAL AND INSIGNIFICANT.   THE COSMOS STRETCH BEYOND SCIENCE
AND IMAGINATION.   I WILL LEAVE MY MARK AND EVENTUALLY IT WITH WITHER.

I will leave my mark even though I know it will wither.
I will leave my mark on others and they will blossom.

I WILL LEAVE MY MARK FOR IT IS MINE TO LEAVE.

you will leave a mark and it will wither.
you will leave a mark and I will blossom.
you will leave a mark.

Descendants

one day, I will have a son
& all this hatred will melt away

when the wicked witch of the west was killed
no one seemed in awe she was made of sugar
her granddaughter does not know the story
of how villagers paraded after her ashes
& caught them on their tongues, like snowflakes
baked cakes with her remains
then loosened their belts with a sigh
because they were so full

some nights, I imagine the devil has cane sugar bones
I lick his kneecaps & my teeth chatter,
shimmy, then dance off my jaw
I wonder why my molars are so eager to leave my mouth empty
—I never wonder why the devil is a man

I whisper my son's name like a prayer
because I hope someday he will save me

after my friend was raped
I pierced my own ears
then threaded them with garnets
I gave myself a new piercing
for each friend who shared their story

the disease had taken root in vein in muscle
even then, I did not kill myself
I did not kill myself because
I could not write a good enough suicide note
that, & I didn't want anyone
to be the one to find my body

tonight, I want to shed my skin
leave it crumpled at the foot of the bed

crawl into a womb of sheets
& wait for a new life

these days, I'd rather think of birth
& right now, I want to be both mother & child

—**Nora Boyle** (she/her)

Everyone Sees Eden
—After *We All Know About Margo* by Megan Pillow

Everyone sees Eden for *what she is.*

Eden, who everyone acknowledges is so pretty *for a girl like her*, has her Taylor Swift tote bag on her right arm and a flannel wrapped around her shoulders. Eden, who wears long sleeves in an unseasonably warm February, who does anything to hide the hair on her arms, is claiming to be cold-natured while she's sweating. Eden, whose skill for layering outfits and reorganizing the wardrobes of girls who never had to struggle to find jeans for their height or shoes for their size is second to none—she's walking to her 11 A.M. lecture and trying not to think of her 4 P.M. meeting. Eden, who's been awake since seven and says it's to make sure she got assigned a room with the only other girl like her on the boy's floor, is really just wondering when the last time she actually slept was.

Eden, who's listening to the same love songs she's been looping since six guys ago, when she first heard that she just "wasn't the right kind of girl," gets a text from Cat about her boyfriend, who everyone knows Eden was rejected by because he doesn't date *girls like her*, and answers in two seconds even though she's been on delivered since yesterday, and everyone knows it bothers her. Everyone sees everything that bothers her.

Everyone's watching Eden, who's been a pro at matching foundation shades since she had to buy her first bottle at fourteen to hide the razor bumps on her neck, as she pulls her phone out and pretends to scroll an empty inbox so she can tilt her head down and hide the redness along her sharp jaw. Eden, who has a dozen step skincare routine and still says she has acne instead of razor burn, brushes past a woman on her way into the bathroom and whispers a small "excuse me." Everyone sees the look in the woman's eyes, and everyone knows Eden whispers because it's the highest her voice can go.

Eden, who kisses girls when she gets drunk so she can convince herself she wants to be with them instead of be them, locks herself in the stall closest to the wall and leans against the cheap gray plastic of the divider to let the last sleepless night catch up to her for a moment. Eden, who didn't say anything when Ashley said, "I'm only kissing girls now, and Eden" when she broke up with her boyfriend, opens her calendar and sees the 4 P.M. slot staring back at her, and everyone knows where she's going and why she's dreading it. Eden, who scrolls past the report she filed at 1 A.M. last Saturday night, looks again at the photos of herself from right before her first frat party. Eden, who told her friends to go home without her from the couch in the room of Duck The Frat Guy, asks one last time if anyone from the party group chat is free to go with her this afternoon, and everyone knows the answer will be silence.

Eden, who finally managed to get out of bed and wash her hair on Monday night, adjusts the brunette strands to frame her face and draw attention away from her jaw. Eden, who never even pulled her pants down before she sat, takes toilet paper off the roll and pretends to wipe and flush in case someone else is in the bathroom. Eden, who has stubble everywhere from the lip down, retucks her shirt and puts her tote bag back on and comes out of the stall after the usual minute of silence that proves no one is in the bathroom. Eden, who looks normal and calm, washes shaking hands in the empty bathroom and waits until she leaves to put her mother's tiger's eye ring back on; anything to get out before someone else comes in.

Eden, who has published award winning poems about womanhood that she feels like she plagiarized, Eden who has defended women's rights in AP government debates even when she was questioned why she cared so much, Eden who learned how to do the makeup she's wearing from drag queens while everyone else shared tips they learned from their moms, Eden who always talks about her womanhood until everyone is looking at her like they want her to shut up, Eden who has watched the time that this takes shrink from five minutes to one, Eden who all the girls say is beautiful but never has a date to any of the football games, Eden who learned how to perfect her eyeliner because she always cried it off, leaves the bathroom and everyone can hear her heart thundering away in her flat chest.

Eden, who hasn't had a mother in six years, who's here on a full ride and still keeps her rejection letter from her Ivy Leagues in her desk, sits in her seat and checks her phone and we all see the empty inbox. Eden, who opens her laptop to take notes and pretends that every vibration from the phone of the girl sitting next to her is her own friends leaping to go with her today, whose first thought of who to tell about Saturday night was an email to her professors about missing Monday's classes, is typing a message to the contact under the office for Title IX and canceling her scheduled follow up. Everyone knows but no one bothers to stop her. Everyone knows nothing would have been done about it anyway. Everyone knows she will be exactly what she always is: quiet.

Eden had asked where the bathroom was at the frat house, and a girl had shown her. She'd used it. Eden had walked home by herself that night, and the frat president swaying drunkenly in the street had watched her go, screaming the words that would haunt her for the rest of her life down the street the entire while. Everyone knows she has been screaming the same words at herself for years, and everyone knows that this was the first time anyone else had said them, and everyone knows what that means. Everyone knows that in ten years she will be a psychologist so she can learn to cope with the words he screamed that are still rattling around in her head, and he will be a lawyer or a politician or a businessman or a doctor and he won't even remember saying them. Eden, who everyone knows will think she sees him in the face of every nondescript blonde man in every grocery store, pharmacy, bank, restaurant and doctor's office for the rest of her life. Everyone knows why, and everyone knows that will include her own reflection. Eden, who everyone sees, Eden who everyone ignores, Eden, Eden, *Eden, who.*

—**Delilah Chamberlain** (she/they)

And so you are in love

Sweet vertigo,
as Earth rolls away below you
paths rise to catch your heel. The night
comes tiptoeing like morning, day

parts her hair, and heaven's eye opens. You
can see through to tomorrow, trace the secret
trails of birds in the air, you know

where the fox goes in the long grass, the patience
of trees. You are learning to speak
all over again. Awash in a melody of Other,
you are the still hub turning

at the middle of the cyclone, the flame
in the tiger's tooth, the skin
on the flanks of Hercules.

No one can hide from you.
Ancestors in photographs
with their backs turned to the camera
reveal the lineaments of their longing
and desire to you, through the stretching
and tension of their muscles.

All your nerves are exposed,
the understanding
shoots through you like sunlight,
as if you had turned into lace.

One look, one word spoken in haste has
made you shiver like a spider's threads
at the breeze of any passing sorrow, the buzz
of any happiness. Like sewing pins

pulled by a magnet, you gather
other lives to you, you add them

to your own fabric, their sorrows
and joys become your own.

—**K Roberts** (they/them)

apricots or women beneath the branches

the rotting became ritual,
as each year
the soft orange fruits
became bruised and seeping,
left decaying on the browning grass.

the supple weight of the summer heat
sucked the life from the apricots,
rotting on the branches of sun soaked trees.
the orchard drowned under the sickly fragrance
of sugars coated in new mold,
the only thing left growing in the scorching heat.
as august dragged on,
the sun spoiled what remained of the apricots.

summer shone brighter and stayed longer that year.
and it dragged more days into itself
in each of the years that followed.
summer slowly swallowed autumn into sunshine
and burned june and july under its blistering sun.

in the long summer,
we spent our days by the ocean,
desperately drenching our skin
underneath the lukewarm respite of the waves.
we caught sturgeon beneath the docks
and drank warm beer.
as we fried our fish against the rocks,
we wished for apricot wine and sweet salsa
to go along with our meals,
and we wished
for our skin to
stop feeling so much like sandpaper.
but we were thankful,
for we were not yet dying—
no,
only rotting.

—**Katie Barlow** (she/her)

Crop Circle

      Crop circle year, slowly coming of age. Thoughts
you didn't know you had, urges that just popped up. When the whole family gathers round to gander, you
stay quiet as a stalk, quiet as dinner at the table.
      Oil lamp year. Dimly lit love burns the farmhouse down. Douse the open flames 'til you're
reminded that
you look the same. Burning, yearning, and a
house-sized crop circle pops up.
      When the whole town gathers round to gander,
you stay quiet as a mother, quiet as dust on the mantle.

—**Odette Augustine** (she/her)

Caught in Waiting

Persephone, Claudius, Ophelia

Sounds rolling
Back and forth, mine the vault
What to name a child?

Rain, Lavender, Meadow

Turn over odds
Assign gender
Names become place become history

Israel, Palestine, America

And it must be on its way
We wait for appearance of blood
Announcement of flesh

Hans, Sophie, Christoph

If language could mute history
We could call our children

Jezebel, Lazarus, Magdalene

—**Chelsea Palermo** (she/her)

Me, Together

On my first day of performing arts high school, I left gym class to hyperventilate in the escalator shaft.

Moments before, I was eavesdropping on two fellow first-years wearing fake band t-shirts from Forever 21 and comparing their respective Broadway experiences. Girl 1 had performed in Matilda; Girl 2 was in Billy Elliot. I was stiff and cross-legged on the glossy basketball court beside them, then suddenly floating above my body, shouting down at my ponytail, "What the fuck are you doing here?"

Half-person-half-ghost, I asked to be excused, darted to the shaft, and tried to focus on the gentle whir of the rotating rubber handrail as I waited to come together again.

The day was a mystifying blur of directions. Once the academic half concluded, the admin sent all drama freshmen to the basement and stuffed us into a small dance studio. The room had mirrored walls on two sides so we could all observe our feebly-veiled panic from several angles at once.

The drama staff, dressed in black, stood in a line facing us as if about to burst into jazz choreography. They waited, quiet and still, as extra-lost students trickled in late. The crowd was dotted with even worse graphic tees and roared with a thousand introductory conversations. I could feel it happening again—that internal separating—until I locked eyes with someone I knew.

***

I didn't particularly like Leo, but his apartment was always well-stocked with snacks, and the party sounded awesome on the invite. In fact, as a ten-year-old, it was the sexiest, most wondrous thing I had ever heard: a Halloween-themed, co-ed, sleepover birthday party. How did he even think of that? The invitation instructed me to arrive in costume.

Dressed as an extremely convincing Darth Vader, wearing a mask attached to a control pad with a voice-changing button, I waved my parents off in the lobby and entered Leo's apartment alone. His mother led me to his room, where the other children played on the floor, wading in a crunchy, rainbow sea of Legos. I cleared a spot for myself on the rug and began accumulating materials for a spaceship.

The boy next to me, Adam, was focused on his own project, which was mostly red and asymmetrical. His techniques impressed me, so, using gestures alone, I proposed we combine efforts. For the next half hour or so, we huddled together and wordlessly secured as many two-by-fours as possible, the most critical piece for robust construction. As we sloshed around in the plastic, I started to overheat and removed my helmet, careful not to whack anyone with the control pad.

"Wait...you're a girl?" Adam gasped.

Everyone looked up: clowns, ballerinas, secret agents. My grip tightened on our franken-ship.

"That's cool," he said. And then, it was time for dinner.

For the rest of the night, Adam and I ignored the Legos and instead constructed our list of things in common: our favorite color, our favorite Pokémon, and even our blood type. I lied the entire time. I hated the color red and didn't know my blood type or what a Pokémon was. Regardless, we made each other laugh so much we pulled our sleeping bags together before bed, and as we drifted off, Adam whispered—

"Do you like me more than a friend?"

I said yes.

But on Monday at school, we didn't speak. We weren't friends; we'd never been in the same class. I occasionally noticed him in the yard or hallways but never waved. Eventually, we were off to different middle schools, and he was a distant, primarily embarrassing, memory.

***

We stared at each other, open-mouthed. Adam was on the other side of the crowd and accidentally stepped on several people on his way to me. We hugged for the first time, quickly and awkwardly. In our embrace, I remembered myself—that I was good at making friends—and felt everything come together again.

We exchanged shock and delight that the other had also always been interested in acting. I didn't remember Adam being so loud—just worldly and self-assured.

A girl with dangly earrings and purple eyeshadow interrupted our reunion.

"Are you guys cousins?"

She was breathy and giggly and only addressing Adam. Later, we would all discover she was a kleptomaniac—her locker was full of people's "lost" shoes—but at the time, she just seemed, at worst, rude. Adam hung on her every word.

The studio had reached critical mass, and our teachers began calling our names to gather their respective thirty-student ensembles for the year. When Adam, my ex-lover, heard his name, he jumped and hooted, and the whole room smiled.

Miss Purple Eyeshadow and I were assigned to Mr. Dalton. He was broad-shouldered, long-haired, and the youngest teacher in the department. He opened his welcome speech with, "They told me I was teaching sophomores. Go figure."

Our classes exited separately. I didn't wave to Adam.

***

That collection of moments in the dance studio was a microcosm of our next four years together. Our high school reeked of two things: The Victoria's Secret body lotion slathered onto all the prettiest girls and the inflated egos of the few straight, *cute-adjacent* boys. At our school and around the city, Adam was infamous for being one of them and also *markedly insane*. He would do anything for a laugh—throw his best friend under the bus, invent outlandish stories, take his pants off, scream as loud as he could on Subway cars, and then look around confusedly.

The only class we ever had together was economics. Adam came in twenty minutes late daily, holding an iced coffee, and was usually high. When he grew bored of the lesson, he would thunderously and abruptly declare, "I'm on fire," before violently thrashing in his seat until Dr. Bendt threatened to phone the office. He never did; Dr. Bendt was understandably scared of Adam.

One time, Adam pretended to forget how to use the stairs, latched onto the backpacks of two tiny freshmen, and pulled them down an entire flight. To his credit, everyone always laughed, but then we would look around at each other like, *Should we stop him? How do we stop him?*

He was amazing to watch on stage and also a complete fuck-up. He flunked gym. He forgot his lines during a big performance and improvised for twenty minutes while his co-stars froze in horror. He never showed up to any of the state-mandated Regents exams. To avoid embarrassment—and for fear my eardrums would burst—I avoided hanging out with him in large groups when he was most emboldened to make a scene.

Alone, though, he was different.

***

In our junior year, I misplaced my student ID. During the morning rush, I tried to sneak through the detectors and past security, but a guard saw me and yanked me backward through the crowd to the dean's office. Mr. Winters was a fat, balding man with droopy eyelids and a cane. At all times, he looked about to keel over and die.

"This one is a troublemaker," the guard spat before slamming the door. I had never been in real trouble before. Mr. Winters looked me up and down, typed my name into the database, and read my lateness record aloud.

"You think you can do whatever you want?" he asked.

I stared down at my boots as Mr. Winters yelled for a few more minutes before sending me to class. I avoided the more popular escalator and took the stairs instead, shuffling slowly and heavily upwards. As I turned onto the fifth-floor landing, I saw Adam sitting alone on the top step, avoiding his English class. He watched as I approached, and before he could greet me, I collapsed beside him and sobbed.

Something about running into him made the tears come quickly, followed by an even more humiliating sputtering. Maybe I was already reliving some childhood memory of being scolded, and Adam only further assured me I was trapped in the past. Or, despite his craziness, his familiarity made me feel safe.

He stayed silent anyway and pressed his hand firmly against my shoulder. I pulled myself back together and nodded once to him before leaving. A few periods later, he picked me up from math class and escorted me back to the basement.

"I just thought I should check on you," he explained on the escalator.

***

Sometimes, we took the F train home. Although we lived opposite directions from our stop, Adam liked walking me to my apartment building so we could laugh together. It was thoughtful laughing, not his usual manic cackle. We would even sit on my front stoop in the spring until it got dark.

Once, he blurted out, "Should we just kiss?"

"No. Definitely not." I laughed. He didn't.

I regret saying that—not because I wanted to kiss him, but because it started something that would never entirely end.

Soon after, Adam invented this bit where he would say goodbye to me at the station, pretend to walk away towards his house, but then turn a corner, run, and hide somewhere along my route. As I approached his hiding spot, he would jump out and scare me. The first time he did it, we laughed so hard we fell on the floor, though my heart was still racing an hour later. When I got home, I noticed indents where I had dug my nails into my palm.

I started to walk home cautiously, now hyper-aware of every alley and dumpster. Sometimes, I was genuinely terrified of Adam. He promised to stop a few times and then scared me anyway, making him laugh the hardest of all. I grew so anxious about it that I insisted he walk me home so I could keep track of him.

We got into a play-fight a block from my house the last time he walked me home. We were shoving each other, half smiling, half frowning, and before I knew it, his hand was around my neck, lifting me off the sidewalk. I couldn't breathe, and I kicked at him until he put me down. With my hand over my throat, I screamed that he was a psychopath, and as I stormed away, he shouted back that I was "overreacting." I think he may have called me a bitch. I couldn't believe being special to him wasn't enough to protect me from his erratic wrath. How could he want to hurt *me*? It kept me up at night.

***

Later that week, I stood before our drama cohort and presented my short film project based on Hamlet's to-be-or-not-to-be soliloquy. Half of my video was silent footage; the other half was pure audio with a black screen. I thought it was a piece of shit until I started explaining my process and everyone's hands shot up. My classmates had so much to say about the piece, and we spent the rest of the period on my work.

I was not in Matilda or Billy Elliot, and I was definitely not the best actor in the department, but that day, I realized I had something to say. Adam looked guilty in the audience. We hadn't spoken since he choked me, and I could feel him missing me.

After the bell rang, he pulled me aside and said sorry, more at his sneakers than me.

"You're really smart," he said.

I was so relieved I teared up as I pulled my winter jacket out of my locker.

***

During my first year of college, someone sent me a Facebook post listing ten boys from NYC, all accused of sexual harassment and assault. Adam was number seven.

For years Adam told me all of his secrets. "Don't repeat this," he would implore before taking a slow breath. Once, he told me, these two girls from the grade below us pressured him into having a threesome with them. Another time, his serious girlfriend gave him a blowjob without his consent. He told me our mutual friend cornered him at a party and said, "If you don't kiss me, I'll cry." He was always the victim, and I was the special-est girl who got to listen and console him.

But staring at that Facebook list, alone in my dorm, I realized Adam had been telling me other people's stories. He was describing other people's pain, which he had inflicted.

I couldn't close my eyes without imagining him on stage, glowing, convincing, lying. I recognized the other listed names too. Did a version of me exist in their stories? Who was I in Adam's story? Who was I in my own?

Adam has a girlfriend now. I've watched them Venmo each other grocery money for five years. I don't know which stories she gets.

I don't miss Adam, but I miss being ten, when I was Darth Vader, when no one wanted to hurt me, when I hadn't ever split in two.

—**Violet Piper** (she/her)

Demons – Lydie Piper (she/her)

Paul takes the form of a mortal jerk

a coworker complains
every time someone tells him

what my pronouns are:
why does it matter if she's not in the room?

I know this because he tells me—
people seem to think it's important I get your pronouns right—

why does it matter if you're not in the room?
he complains about other things &

uses the same exact excuse—*that slur*
doesn't affect anyone in the direct vicinity—

some slurs are more problematic
than others—language is always changing,

why does it always have to be policed—
why are they keeping track of every mistake I make—

how to tell him he's making himself
into a victim—they aren't out to get him—

they're trying to respect me—
to remind him so he doesn't fuck up

in front of me—*I never use your pronouns*
when you're in the room—how to tell him

THAT ISN'T TRUE—JUST THE OTHER DAY
YOU CALLED ME SHE—but *really*

I'm not out to get you—how to tell him
the committee wants evidence

of the life I lead—that his wrong moves
could be detrimental to me—

I hope if I ever offend anyone, they'll just say so—
I don't intend to do any harm—

how to tell him
he has harmed me

—**Alexandra Servey** (they/them)

Infinity

carrying the burden of heavy shoes
so big my heel keeps slipping out,
I run up the hill, a moss forest bath
welcomes me, green reflection of water
I am not as fast as I was prior to bearing life
swaying my wide hips in infinity circles
as yellow earth and red sun made the silver moon
smile in the sparkling blue sky of day, colourful
Tibetan prayer flags and a copper mood ring
left at an altar to the mountain Gods
golden eagles hover, circling white for
their morning meal as blisters
form with the repetitive chafing
of inheritance

—Rina Malagayo Alluri (she/her)

When we die, can we become mycelium?

In constant communication?

A new form of regeneration?

I hope your consciousness remains a constant companion. This is not quiet reincarnation, but unbecoming to become intertwined with what already exists.

My shoulders used to shudder at the thought of smoldering into ash or being packed beneath 2,597 pounds of earth. Now I hope we are devoured by the same worm colony, deposited in the same soil, that we sprout the same mushrooms, feed the same flowers; to nourish into eternity.

Our hearth has become my heaven and our dirt is the afterlife being tended to today.

—**Maggie Bowyer** (they/he)

River Muse – Kathleen Baker (she/her)

Like throwing your self at a vanishing point

The lead up was waiting / every month and minute long / and in the last days / waiting with a tight belly under a tight shirt at the county fair / standing in line for a funnel cake / and waiting at the parade / wondering if this was the last thing I'd ever do alone / with zombies marching by / and later the local mothers complained / the undead! they eat people! evil! not in front of my children! / and I wondered if that was something I could get mad about, too, one day / watching the guys from the car wash and the community college dressed in torn sweats and jeans / their faces white / abs tight / and eyes ringed in black / stomping down Main Street / dancing to Thriller / I waited in the quiet nursery we made / curled up on the couch as each body part started to give up one at a time / back ached / belly button popped / hips pulled apart / and even my face—it froze! / the last supper at home was fries dipped in a frosty that dripped down my chin / and then I stretched across three chairs in the waiting room just to hear a doctor say it's time / to / separate / the mother / from the baby / in the emergency room I waited / for my lover to become a father / to fill out the forms, / call the insurance / I waited for a patch to be taped over my eye / which had stopped blinking / the quitter / one half of my mouth had stopped smiling / and I waited for the pulses to get closer / to bend me over / for someone to say this was really happening / then when it seemed like the waiting was over/ water broken / every peak seizing me around the back / wrapping its squeeze around me / clamping down / I bounced I breathed I gasped / tried every trick a girl knows / joked / I floundered / who knows how to move / to get away from the pain / was it in a squat / was it in the shower with the water pounding my ass / was it on the toilet / in the bed / when I felt I might die / I was a baby / crying / separated from The Mother they said I had to be now / where was the way away from the pain / he said, *you become an acorn of pain at each one / in an agony shell and I can t get to you to help* / and I called it / said call 'em for the drip / and we waited / the nurse held me on her chest / as the needle went in / she had been waiting for me to cave / and then I slept / fuzzy as a drunk / waiting for this thing / a being? / to scoot down my pelvic bones / fit her head into the lock / and make me care about things like zombies and being strong / after two hours / we played quiet music from our youth and everyone hushed / it's like a sit up / like a push you can't feel / it's like throwing your self into a vanishing point / it's time / and you're so close / she's! / here's the top of her head / here she comes / here she is / here she is / look at her / listen to her cry / squint in the light / wrap her waxy fingers around mine / hi / I said in a mother's voice / for the first time.

—**Sara Triana** (she/her)

The Author Lets You in on a Secret

The morning likes to shine
a light on all the dark parts
of me I'm too afraid to let
anyone else see.

I unpick the scabs
on my skin & I make
the bed fresh before
you come over.

Every breath I take for love
is an exit wound,
my lungs are a dreary night
& you are an umbrella.

The dull ache against my
persistent & hardened shell
makes me softer than I want.
Softer than I care to be.

After a while even the
butterflies & eye contact
becomes another chore,
a burden against your back.

Text "wya" even when I
know you're across the bar
& thank god when I see
you open it with a smile.

My impatience with love
used to only burden me.

What I mean by that is
everyone seems to be on
the tracks with a destination
to someone else

& I am already at the station
looking around at an
empty platform asking myself
am I too early or too late?

—**Gabriel Noel** (he/him)

First published by BarBar Publishing

For Eve

Something full of shame and hemlock troubles me to ask Eve for her forgiveness. Age has skewed my sight. I see her in blinding, starry-eyed stained glass, at last.

A snake slithering restless with compassion. A man's heart bursting with so much devotion that he never once misses his other rib. Half a lifetime at her side. All those who wander into her darkness will meet banishment and decay. All the misconceptions in the flesh. All the reasons I cannot blame her.

God will see me kiss her hands, her thighs. Please her for praise and repentance. I will listen to her list her wicked ways—in moans and between sighs. I will spell my sins out with my tongue.

God will have to crawl to me for forgiveness.

—**Odette Augustine** (she/her)

The ones whose names are forgotten

They eat atmospheres
Taste feelings in the air
Feel the vibration of sound
Before it is heard
See shapes shadows spectres
Weave dreams into worlds
Call futures into being
Through the warps in time.

Felt at twilight when the mist comes down
A presence, more sensed than seen
Electricity in the air
Frisson in the water
Hiding in plain sight
You will not hear them unless they want you to

—**Amanda Ball** (she/her)

the thought vomit of a femme because i can only write about being a lesbian

it's as if i found that narrow fellow wrapped around my ankle
twisted vines over a grave
and ivy swarms my veins

i should crumble like a brick wall
armpit hair brittle as a witch
but nobody really knows i'm a lesbian

and yes my mother believes i am a hippie
god forgotten junkie
or maybe even a criminal behind rusted bars

instead my neck is on a stake
and my body lay in a puddle below me
for the queers to lap up my blood

how to erase the crooked smiles of men
their drooping old mouths that tell me to smile.
father, forgive them, for they know not what they are doing.

and maybe i don't only write about being a lesbian, i write about god
but i would hope he liked the attention
the way small voices ascend him to heaven
while rings clatter to my nightstand. blessed be.

—**Abigail Cain** (they/she)

I am the reaper and the ghost

I sit across from a Spector in therapy. She whispered I was her Angel with conviction, shared a story of falling into heaven three times over and God reaching toward her through my hands, sending her back to her skeleton with the statement I AM NOT FINISHED WITH YOU YET. She says I was her Angel but every time I take a vacation it ends with a funeral.

I FEAR RESTING MEANS THEIR DEATH BUT CONTINUING THIS WAY MEANS MY OWN. I FEAR PHONE CALLS AND HANDWRITTEN NOTES. I FEAR OPEN GARAGE DOORS AND LATE OCTOBER. I FEAR MY OWN DEMISE BUT I FEAR LIFE MORE.

I sit across from a computer screen, a new therapist, and an urn I dug up from the back of my closet. She doesn't whisper anymore. She knows my fingers slip right through her and I know her fists have lost their weight. She whispers I am not finished with you yet through the gaps in my processing.

you might not be done haunting me, but I am done living with phantoms. pain without acceptance can only lead to suffering. I am a ghost and the reaper, I bring death on sabbatical and befriend the familiar monster. they share their burdens and I add each one to my burning regrets. we roast marshmallows and pretend we don't hear the shrieking. my skin tingles with terror too often, but I let the seaside breeze brush it away. I fear midday and the end of summer and the chill of winter and cursive letters and unknown callers and funerals, but as we split s'mores I see how we can coexist.

—**Maggie Bowyer** (they/he)

Calling Katherine

When we strolled through our hometown at seventeen, lamplit sidewalk turning slick in the winter's first snow, we were reenacting a mystery. Thirty-six years earlier, in November of 1974, a college freshman was snatched from the streets on her walk back to campus. Weeks after her disappearance, on Thanksgiving, two unsuspecting hunters found her naked body set atop an old stone wall. She was draped in a red coat, the color of maple leaves just before they drop.

My friends and I learned about Katherine from our parents and grandparents, who after drinking too much liquor shared their theories about creepy neighbors and serial killers. Speculating was easier than facing the fear that festered in our community as years, then decades, passed without an arrest.

A few miles into the hills surrounding town, my friend Dee's mom ran a salon in the back room of a farmhouse. She had blonde wispy hair and dark fluttery lashes—a mirror image of the models in her beauty magazines stacked on the coffee table. Outside the salon, twilight settled into the acres of farmland surrounding us, and I longed for someplace more fitting to the cosmopolitan woman I hoped to become. The last client went home and Dee and I jumped into the squishy black chairs to take turns coiffing one another's heads with sticky clouds of hairspray. We lined our lips in brown pencil, dabbed shimmer onto our cheekbones. We believed that attractiveness was a currency we could barter for worth.

Growing up in the shadow of an unsolved murder, we should've been the kinds of high school girls who always went exactly where we said we were going. Instead, we perfected our lies and dove headfirst into the darkness. We lit up as soon as the stars blinked on over our valley, speeding along winding county routes toward bonfires in distant pastures. Once, we pitched a tent in a hilltop graveyard and stayed there until sunrise. By the time we sneaked back into our homes and dozed off at dawn, our dreams were tainted with the sounds of that night's rebellion—a coyote's sharp cry, the crack of beer cans, twigs snapping underfoot. We had an unspoken agreement: To escape our destiny of wounded women, wives, and mothers, we had to be fearless.

Our fascination with other realms began with Goosebumps and The Blair Witch Project. Soon, we were making ouija boards from pizza boxes and scrawling on letters with black marker, grease stains spotting the cardboard. There was only a field between Dee's house and the stone wall where Katherine's body was found, so the prospect that we could summon her ghost into the bedroom didn't seem far-fetched.

One day sitting cross-legged on her pink shag carpet with the lights off, shaky fingers touching the planchette, we got up the nerve to try.

Katherine—who hurt you?

Katherine—what do you know that we don't?

We tried again and again to contact her, but all we got were jumbled messages from other lost souls who hadn't known her either. I took it to mean that Katherine's spirit wasn't there anymore, that she was finally at peace. I couldn't have known she would always be haunting me.

We pulled on push-up bras and swallowed birth control and changed our hair with boxed dye from Walmart, too naïve to see that participating in the system objectifying us would just weaken our self-efficacy. Conflating male attention with power meant our humanity became an afterthought, even to ourselves. Eventually, there were many ways we learned that this is a mistake: backed into the walk-in freezer of a pizza restaurant, knife to our throat; grabbed from a moving bicycle and tackled to the concrete; groomed by a teacher who said we'd look beautiful in his bed; gaslit into believing we did not catch our husband cheating in our house; shoved from an upstairs window, our children crying *mommy!* the last thing we heard.

As I neared adulthood, the gazes that had made me giddy with self-importance began to ignite my fear response. Everywhere there were strangers hungry for us, their hovering moon faces and clouds of ragged breath a storm we couldn't outrun. Those years driving around doing exactly what we wanted, disillusioned by our youth and freedom—wasn't Katherine's killer still out there? What if he waited at the edge of a firelit cornfield, waiting until one of us stumbled onto his path? We deserved to be unafraid. But maybe the reason we kept our lives is because nobody decided to take them.

When I say Katherine haunts me, I mean I can't help but imagine her final moments. If, in those hopeful seconds, she believed she could be saved by someone who loved her. An old boyfriend bursting through the door; her mother calling the police just in time. How the air turned sour then, the sentence clear in his eyes. Right before the lights went out, she saw that no one was coming.

Today, my hometown is both foreign and ripe with memory. There are new drugstores and strangers filling their aisles, and yet, I see us in the teens giggling at the gas station; hear us in voices bouncing across the gorge. In these rooms of history, part of me will always be wandering those dark, wet streets with Katherine and Dee and the girls I knew, a cold frost dusting our shoulders while we ask the unseen world for answers.

—**Michelle Polizzi** (she/her)

if I saw a poem by Joseph, hypothetically

sometimes I look up and see
the candelabra hanging
above Joseph's head;
large jewels fastened
with copper wire
in soft motions
and I wonder
were they carefully picked
by the Maker or factory
produced with bumps
and scratches as witness

I made the same assumption
historically, that I was the only
trans person walking into the room,
that his name soothed,
that he fondly remembers
a parent whispering it;
without the nightmares
of a name unheard in decades
intended to be yours
shouted as birth down the hall

that the screws
in the ceiling,
that the hinges
on each joint,
will hold.
maybe he has been
unscrewing them at night
when nobody is looking

—**Wilfred Jensen** (they/them)

Snapshot

Daydreams
Pick me up like thistledown
Drop me in different worlds
With an underlying soundtrack

I catch myself
An Alice lucid dreaming
Falling through mirrors
Into bottomless pools

Watching images
Come to focus
Like sluiced celluloids
In a darkened room

Where ectoplasmed eyes
Stare back
Through the window
Of another world

—**Amanda Ball** (she/her)

Dear Ms. Gordon

Dear Ms. Gordon

Congratulations on getting the part of Mayella Ewell in this professional production of *To Kill a Mockingbird*. Your audition was outstanding. You really brought to the table a level of psychological abuse and daddy issues that we did not see from the other actors vying for this role. You were not afraid to be ugly, raw, and completely unhinged.

Bravo

We did want to say that we took notice of you and another actor at the auditions. Talking too close, tucked in a corner "running lines". We saw the way you touched his arm while you laughed. We saw the way he stared at your ass when you went up to the stage for your monologue. It was all so gross and obvious that it was, well...sad.

We wanted to inform you that he was also cast in this play in the role of Heck Tate, the sheriff. Talent is talent after all, even with questionable morals. Though his part is a supporting role, he will show up to every rehearsal, even though he may not be needed on stage.

This will be confusing to you.

We also want to say that we know about what happened when you met him two years ago. He was playing Oedipus, and you were playing his daughter Antigone.

Your father was dying, but not dead...not yet.

Soon.

Your father came to the theatre, he saw you on stage. Then he was gone. A theatre ghost light did not stop this from haunting you.

There is an irony here, or maybe symbolism—you know this, and we know this.

But no one will talk about it now.

Though your friendship with this actor was *almost* platonic, we remember that one kiss, just as you were packing up your dressing room.

Antigone. Dirty, dirty daughter.

We also remember the day you met in the park to run lines, then ate grilled cheese at a diner...his second son had been born just a month before and you were falling in love with an idea that would never be real. Dummy.

That said, bravo on it just being one kiss.

We wish you luck during this next production, two weeks of rehearsal and two months of shows. We understand you will have plenty of time to reconnect and hope you do so responsibly. We would hate for this to affect either of your family life, and most of all we would hate it to affect the production.

When you see *him*, please make sure to ask about his wife and his children—be polite, Antigone. Be a good girl, a good daughter. Do not ask if he is happy, and do not tell him you are not.

xxoo

PS – sorry to hear about your father's death. I hope this *does* affect your performance in this show.

Dear Ms. Gordon

The person in your life that you pretend to love on the outside, loves you on the inside. He loves you. He is kind. He is beautiful. He is better for you than—

Oh, I am sorry, is it too late?

It is too late.

Xoxo

Dear Ms. Gordon

Flirting is not cheating. It's okay to tell yourself this but it is not okay at *this* moment to believe it.

It has come to our attention that at night before you fall asleep you have started to wonder if his sons have his eyes. You wonder about their skin. They live near the ocean. You wonder if their little baby faces are already aging. You wonder if their cheeks are plump with tough, reddened skin and laughing crinkles in the corner of their eyes.

You cannot have children. You should be sad about this, but it is another one of the many things that you have chosen not to feel anything about.

Xxoo

Dear Ms. Gordon

It's done. It's happened.

You will pretend that the first time that you and "Heck Tate" finally fucked, that it's love. You will ignore that he took you to the place where he worked because he had the security code. He worked at a robotics firm that had a *fun office* with bean bag chairs and black lights.

It's not love. Except we know you think it is. It's just an orgasm. He looks like George Clooney and Dennis Quaid, and he is older than you, of course he is. They always are.

xxoo

PS – again, really sorry about what happened to your dad, those last days, when he begged you to put a pillow over his face. It's good you didn't do it. There are plenty of things you will need to forgive yourself for, that should not be one of them.

Dear Ms. Gordon

Congrats! You lost 14lbs during the run of this show. You are proud of that, and if you are honest, you are proud of all of it. Your performance, your secret dressing room blow jobs. You are proud that the person everyone had a crush on has been inside of you. You are proud of biting his fingers so hard while you came that you tasted his blood. We saw you when he wanted to see you touch yourself, blood still drying on your chin.

xo

Dear Ms. Gordon

His wife was at the cast party. On a stage of actors with bags under their eyes and smudged makeup—she wore corduroys and a fleece vest. The theatre was cold. She drank expensive craft beer. An IPA? A stout? You don't drink beer, and this is not the flex you think it is. You were in a pleather skirt with no panties because this is what *he* wanted.

Your crotch was freezing; you wished there had been heat in the theatre. You wished you were back under the stage lights, a thousand people thinking you were anyone except who you are.

He didn't make eye contact with you the entire night.

You stared at them across the room. His hand on the small of her back. His thumb making small loving circles against fuzzy fleece fabric. They finished each other's sentences, and they looked so right together.

You are just murky darkness in the corner of their lives. A shadow hoping to become a real girl. You wondered if your future stepsons would look more like him or her, but you couldn't quite picture it anymore.

Their cheeks.

Their little laughing eyes.

xoxo

PS – he will never leave her, and those boys are ghosts that will never haunt your house. They will only ever haunt you.

—**Jennifer Anne Gordon** (she/they)

Icarus's Daughter***

At 17 my Pa
surrendered to
family & blazed
a black bag
in the smoke
he saw his hidden
rubber breasts
& heels char

a soup of gowns
Mazatlan's pride
& he returned to his Pa
who thanked his fists—
God's manifest—
still dripping in Pa's
okay please i'll stop
the doe-eyed plead
deadened the
dinner table
axed by man

at 17 I held the
bitter taste of Pa's
calcined self-betrayal
only to cast it off
at night by edging
sidewalks to
record my hands
under father
less boys
& because
I am my Pa's son
I drudge a bag
of futures I tried
burning but
the night called

I went out
with razors beneath
my tongue for

borrowed smiles
stroked inside rose bushes
shaped by strangers
passing through my
cupid's bow like ghosts
trapped inside lanterns
hung beside wind chimes
to deny this scared son's
first crawl through closets
chipped in barbwire

the boy glues his forehead
to my finger & in between
shaky swallows his mother
leaks from shut eyes—
he floods me back to Pa's
drunken face dimly lit
flushed by meds
I am not a ma
escapes his clutched
lip smacked against
grandpa's urn

the boy finishes before
I sink the glint of
teeth a reward
for hands foamed
with generational
vengeance I won't
wash myself of &
he laughs Pa he stares
at your daughter & we lose

the patted tap on
this J is the moonlight
to Pa slumped over
my half-finished sink in
Ma's dress mashing
pigments to go back
his missed youth

flashes out pasts
steeped in no thank yous
the grayed tile his
scratched record
as his heels scream
Icarus Icarus Icarus
in front of my vanity

outside the driveway
I stuff my pants with
that boy's hopes downstairs bracing
myself & click
the door's lock
Pa's thud sprints
him to my arms
I become the
seatbelt to Pa's
carcass as he casts
off his masculinity
in my mother's dress
his now daughter
discovers fathers
are mirrors too

***

at 17 my father died
he died at 17
in that bag
at 17 family
became my
father's sun
at 17 I stopped
being a son
at 17 I chose that bag
over family
at 17 I killed my father

—**Alé Cota** (they/she)

acorn as areola

he roots on my right breast
hungry and wanting

i know the milk is coming
electricity trickles through fat and lymph

circles into my areola
drips into my bra

a crop circle in the cotton
seen from space

patterns communicating
what is already in us

arteries and neurons
galaxies

annual rings
repeating

when i was a child i would climb trees
speak to the fairies living in the bark
imagine i was an irish peasant with a tan apron
an english servant walking the moors

always servitude and magic
repetition

now, i wipe the kitchen counters in waves
breathe circles into the early morning air

my contractions a strawberry burst
pain and joy as he crowned

and sunlight
there is that

as an acorn holds the whole of the tree
sprout to decay

he moves to the left breast
roots
and eats

—Ashley Howell Bunn (she/they)

I saw the knowing arrive, wonderful and terrible – Maggie Bowyer (they/he)
—After Alix E. Harrow

white white white
her ashen face as she passed me the keys
see you at home
bleached chalky pallor
tissues on every surface   their little tufts all
white white white caps crashing   drowning
out the news   blurry
transparency
my vision is white and my hands are the same ivory as hers
pulling every book off the shelf   blank pages
all white all pure all clean all empty
white white white   is too loud
smash the entire bookcase on the plywood floor
too light   too bright   too harsh
my sobs shatter the   stillness   in the air
the holiness the merriment the celebration
it is all erased with the words
there was an accident
everything disappeared
it was your mom
I ceased to exist as anything except destruction
colorless and ghostly
white white white
why why why
I know I will feel better tomorrow
how how how
I will feel worse tomorrow
when when when
I saw the flurries even if the weather channel contradicts me

ABOUT THE CONTRIBUTORS

❖ **Abigail Cain** (they/she) is an undergraduate student pursuing literary studies. Her work centers around lesbianism and religious trauma. She has poems published in the Shippensburg University journal, The Reflector.

❖ **Alé Cota** (they/she) is a trans Latiné poet. She holds a B.A. from Carleton College in Latin American and Gender Studies. They explore queer and trans experiences, nostalgia, and the poetics of violence within intimate, familial structures.

❖ **Alexandra Servey** (they/them) has their MFA in Creative Writing. They work mainly in the genre of poetry. Their manuscript *eggs* was a finalist for the National Poetry Series 2023. Servey currently resides in Philadelphia with their lover.

❖ **Alexis Telyczka** (she/her) is an NJ-based artist and writer. Her work can be found on www.alexistelyczka.com, as well as in previous issues of Ember Chasm Review (now Suburbia Journal), The Athena Review, Pinky Thinker Press, and The Closed Eye Open.

❖ **Allister Nelson** (she/her) is a Pushcart Prize-nominated, queer author whose work has appeared in The British Fantasy Society, Apex Magazine, Eternal Haunted Summer, Luna Station Quarterly, Prismatica, etc. Find her work at allisternelson.com.

❖ **Amanda Ball** (she/her) started writing poetry again during the covid pandemic and has had several pieces published in small literary mags. She is currently studying for an MLitt in Creative Writing at the University of Glasgow

❖ **Angela Gabrielle Fabunan** (she/her/hers) is the author of Young Enough to Play (University of the Philippines Press, 2022). She teaches creative writing at Silliman University. She lives with her husband in Small House in Dumaguete City, Philippines.

❖ **Ashley Howell Bunn** (she/they) completed her MFA in poetry through Regis University and holds a MA in Literature from Northwestern University. Their chapbook, in coming light, was published in 2022 by Middle Creek Publishing. They live in Denver, CO.

❖ **Azaliyah Molina** (she/they) graduated from Lehman College with a degree in Creative Writing. They're a Puerto Rican writer from the Bronx. Their work has been featured in the Latino Book Review and Free Verse Revolution Issue XII, Ancestors.

❖ **Carly Popenko** is an emerging writer whose work has been featured in the Hamilton Fringe Festival (Best of Venue award), the HamilTEN Theatre Festival, Kelp Literary Journal, and Running Wild Press - Short Story Anthology, Volume 7.

❖ **Cat Speranzini** (she/her) is an Emerson College alumna. She self-published a full poetry collection titled "Watercolor Souls" in January of 2024. In addition to poetry, she writes flash fiction and is working on a novel.

❖ **Chase Olsen** is an author from central Iowa. He writes fiction featuring LGBT+ characters that encounter real life issues against a fictitious and sometimes fantastical backdrop.

❖ **Chelsea Palermo** is a poet, intuitive & alchemist. She holds an MFA in Poetry from Drew University & was nominated Poet Laureate of Asbury Park, NJ. Her poems can be found in This Broken Shore, Ghost City Review, Soup Can & more. www.chelseapalermo.com

❖ **Chelsie Blair Nunn** (they/them) is an artist and educator working in Knoxville, TN.

❖ **Cheryl Tan** (she/her) is a bisexual Singaporean. A Singapore National Poetry Competition winner, her work has been nominated for the 2023 Pushcart Prize, and her chapbook "Goddess" is forthcoming on Querencia Press.

❖ **Chriss Locker** (they/them) is a nonbinary, neurodivergent author with work currently in new words {issue four} from new words {press} and the TRANS DAY OF VISIBILITY (vol.3 & 4) zine from Sam & Devorah Trans Mentor Project.

❖ **Dante Émile** (he/they) is a gay, transmasculine, Mexican poet currently based in Barcelona – although in the process of fulfilling their lifelong dream of moving to Paris. Whenever he's not writing he's reading articles about niche subjects, discovering new bookshops, drinking too much coffee, and spending time with his cats. His work has been featured in Defunkt Magazine, Sunday Mornings at the River, From Heart to Stomach Magazine, Not Deer Magazine, and various local zines. *Misplaced Organs & Various Saints* is their first collection of poetry.

❖ **Dean Jones** (he/they) is a queer writer and yoga teacher living a life of longing in Hudson NY.

❖ **Delilah Chamberlain** (she/they) is a nineteen-year-old transgender woman from small-town South Mississippi who grew up with more than her fair share of hardship and chose to channel it through a big vocabulary and a bigger heart to put it on the page.

- **Devon Webb** (she/her) is an award-winning writer & editor based in New Zealand, with work published extensively worldwide. She is a founding member of The Circus (@circuslit), a collective prioritising radical inclusivity within the indie lit scene.

- **Elwyn V.J Roth** (they/them) is a disabled transmasc writer. They focus on the body they were stuck in and the changes they choose to make to it. As a poet first, everything they write is imbued with lyrical prose and a sense of poetic irony.

- **Emily Carlson** (she/they) is the author of four poetry chapbooks including Why Misread a Cloud (Tupelo Press, 2022), and I Have a Teacher (The Center for Book Arts, 2016). Their hybrid memoir, Majestic Cut, is forthcoming from Fernwood Press.

- **ena ganguly** (she/they) is a 1.5-generation South Asian writer, poet, and editor. Her work focuses on collective memory, grief, and sensuality. Their work has been featured in KUT Austin, The Austin Chronicle, COURIER, and Prizer Arts & Letters.

- **Fern Roush** (they/them+she/her) writes and teaches experimental poetry*, between mutual aid and long-distance hiking. They have tutored and mc'd Open Mics at the Evergreen Writing Center, and their work has appeared in the Cultivating Voices Pride Poetry March, Slightly West, The Cooper Point Journal, and the Mobile Moon Coop Zine. Find her at moonlitfern.com ***hint**: it's all poetry.

- **Gabriel Noel** (he/they) is a Pushcart Prize nominated poet who received his Bachelor's for Theatre Arts and English at Salem State University. Gabriel's work has previously been featured by Arachne Press, Jelly Bucket Journal, New Note Poetry, Moonstones Art Center, new words {press}, and BarBar Publishing. Gabriel lives on the occupied land of Naumkeag ("fishing place") colloquially known as Salem, Massachusetts and likes to spend time with his partner, go to concerts, make art, read, and go to karaoke bars. You can find more of Gabriel's poetry on Instagram at @peachpitpoetry.

- **hamsa fae** (she/they) is a trans poet and performance artist who is native to Los Angeles. Her poetry book, Blood Frequency, was shortlisted by C&R Press and DVAN in 2022. She has publications in diaCRITICS, Vănguard, new words {press}, Yale School of Environment, Fruitslice, and the Paris 2024 Olympics.

- **Hannah Rowell** is a graduate of Bowling Green State University. She majored in creative writing. She is located in Ohio against her will, and tends to write about loneliness and unconditional love.

- **Irina Tall (Novikova)** is an artist, graphic artist, illustrator. The first personal exhibition "My soul is like a wild hawk" (2002) was held in the museum of Maxim Bagdanovich.

- **Izabella Harvey** is a graduate Counseling student at Walden University. She studied English and Psychology at Queens University of Charlotte. She loves to garden and illustrate. She is currently working on a novel.

- **Jason Clemmons** (he/him) is a Tar Heel poet whose writing reflects his experience as a gen x, gay man in the US South. He lives in central North Carolina with his husband, Peter.

- **Jennifer Anne Gordon** (she/they) was born a strange, pale, and quiet child, a ghost scared of ghosts. She is an actress, artist, writer, & dancer. She haunts lonely places in New Hampshire, though she is not dead. www.JenniferAnneGordon.com

- **Jennifer Renk** (she/her) is a twenty-two year old artist based in Pittsburgh, Pennsylvania.

- **Joanne Le Grove** is a queer woman, currently a full time student at Leeds Beckett university studying creative writing. Her writing has helped her cope with many mental health issues and finally accepting her sexuality. Joanne is also an avid photographer.

- **Jordan Nishkian** (she/her) is an Armenian-Portuguese writer based in California. Her prose and poetry explore themes of duality and have been featured in national and international publications.

- **K Roberts** (they/them) is a professional non-fiction writer, published artist, and first reader for two magazines publishing experimental prose. See more at Decolonial Passage, Xinachtli Journal, Isotrope, Writing in a Woman's Voice, and Axon: Creative Expressions.

- **Kate Warrington** (she/her) is a queer Brooklyn-based writer whose work seeks to explore the intersections of identity and culture. Her writing has appeared in places including HuffPost, Fruitslice and Pangyrus, among others. Find her at katewarrington.substack.com or @warrington_kate

- **Kathleen Baker** (she/her) believes space, time, shape, and pattern create and maintain connections among us all. She has become an ally through the incredible talent, wisdom, and honesty of her students in Environment, Geography, and Sustainability at Western Michigan University.

- **Kathy Bruce** (she, her) is a visual artist based in Upstate New York and Argyll & Bute Scotland. Her work explores archetypal female forms within the context of poetry, literature and the natural environment. Instagram: @kat2bruce & @Kat10bruce

- **Katie Barlow** (she/her) is a midwestern poet and novelist. Her work has been published or is forthcoming in a number of small publications, including Beyond Words Literary Magazine. Her writing can be found @epiloguepoetry on Instagram.

- **Krista Beucler** (she/her) is currently pursuing an MFA in creative writing from Drexel University. Krista's work has been published in Kelp Journal, Mulberry Literary, and South 85 Journal. Her work is forthcoming from Running Wild & RIZE press. Find her at https://kristabeucler.com/

- **L. Lois** (she/her) lives in an urban hermitage where trauma-informed themes flow during walks by the ocean. Her essays have appeared in the Globe and Mail, her recent poetry In Parentheses and Woodland Pattern.

- **L. Noelle McLaughlin** is a ghostwriter based out of New Paltz, New York. In 2024 her writing was featured in The Sunlight Press, and in an anthology by Moonstone Press. lnoellemclaughlin.com

- **Lael Cassidy** goes by she/her. Her work has appeared in Headline Poetry and Press, Silver Birch, Underwood Press, and Beyond Words. She lives in Seattle, teaches writing, and is currently at work on a memoir. You can find her at www.laelcassidy.com.

- **Lauren Kalstad** (she/her) is a poet and essayist. Her work has appeared or is forthcoming in The Passionfruit Review, Thimble Literary Magazine, World Literature Today, and Edible. She lives in Dallas with her husband, daughter, and dog.

- **Liam Strong** (they/them) is the queer author of Everyone's Left the Hometown Show (Bottlecap Press, 2023).

- **Lydie Piper** is a poet and writes Young Adult fiction. She's older and smarter than she appears. She owns a mean dog and prefers pie over cake. Her love language is gift giving and she reads tarot cards.

- **Maggie Bowyer** (they/he) is a proud cat parent and the author of various poetry collections including *Homecoming* (2023) and *When I Bleed* (2021). They've been published in Chapter House Journal, The South Dakota Review, Wishbone Words, and more. Find their work on Instagram @maggie.writes

- **Mary Binninger** (she/her) is a bisexual writer from New York City. She's had poems published online and in-print, in journals such as SUNY Purchase's Sub Mag and Gutter Mag, in addition to Empyrean Literary Magazine, Crystal Crush Mag, and Grim & Gilded Magazine. More of her literary work can be found on Instagram, @marysmanuscripts.

- **Maya Collins** is a published author, passionate artist, and member of the Girls Write Now Collaboratory. Her queer identity and multicultural background inform her work. She currently lives in Pennsylvania and plans to continue her undergrad at Wheaton College in the fall.

- **Melissa Eleftherion** (she/they) is a writer, a librarian, and a visual artist. Born & raised in Brooklyn, they are the author of two poetry collections, field guide to autobiography (The Operating System, 2018), & gutter rainbows (Querencia Press, 2024), and twelve chapbooks including abject sutures (above/ground press, 2024). Melissa now lives in Northern California where she manages the Ukiah Branch Library, curates the LOBA Reading Series, and serves as Poet Laureate Emeritus of the City of Ukiah. Recent work is available at www.apoetlibrarian.wordpress.com.

- **Michelle Polizzi** (she/her) is an essayist and storyteller based in Denver. Her writing has appeared in The Huffington Post, Insider, Bitch, and HerStry, among others. Her memoir, MODEL HOME, is about the housing crisis in rural America.

- **Nora Boyle** is a bookbinder, poet, and witch who runs a small literary press, Lady Book Witch Press. Interested in what it means to craft a material poem, Nora's work explores the intersections of witchcraft, poetry, and bookmaking. Drawing on her feminist and nature-based values, Nora creates dark and whimsical books that simultaneously soothe and unsettle readers. In addition to her Lady Book Witch Press publications, Nora's poetry has been published by Folklore for Resistance, Capsule Stories Magazine, NERVE, Free Verse Revolution, Scumbag Press, Broken Spells Zine, & Folktales Literary Journal. You can see more of her work at: www.ladybookwitchpress.com & on instagram @ladybookwitch.

- **Patricia Feinman** is a writer and a visual artist living in the Catskill mountains. Patricia's first book, VOICES OF THE SEA, a dream series, published by Querencia Press, combines pastel and charcoal drawings with a tone poem depicting a nuclear family's dark search in which dream and reality collide.. LOSING ART, a memoir, will be published by Running Wild/RIZE Press in 2026. Currently, she's working on a novel, MINUS ONE, a coming of age story focusing on three generations of damaged, self-loathing, alcoholic/drug-addicted women. To see more of Patricia's work, please visit patriciafeinman.com

- **Rina Malagayo Alluri** (she/her) is of Indian and Filipina heritage, was raised in Ibadan, Nigeria and migrated to Vancouver, BC, Canada (Turtle Island). She is a peace scholar, yoga practitioner and mother to two headstrong children.

- **Ro Smith** (they/them) is a writer, artist, and dog parent. Their writing centers communities of nonhumans, humans, and the lands in which they encounter one another. They are currently imagining non-anthropocentric languages for creating art.

- **Romy Rhoads Ewing** (she/they) is a writer from Sacramento, California. Their work appears/is forthcoming in HAD, BRAWL, Bullshit Lit, Major 7th Magazine, Nowhere Girl Collective, Y2K Quarterly, MEMEZINE, fifth wheel press, Anti-Heroin Chic, persephone's fruit, Open Ceilings Magazine, and Genrepunk Magazine. Her debut chapbook, "please stay," was published in 2024.

- **Rowan Miller** (she/her) is a queer writer from Providence, Rhode Island. Her poetry intertwines identity and raw emotion, highlighting life's hidden depths and advocating for LGBTQ+ visibility.

- ❖ **Sara Triana** is a poet and artist. She explores themes of parenthood, the climate crisis, embodiment, doubt/hope, and the natural world. She is the author of two children's books, *Love Love Bakery* and *Every Day is Making Day*, and a poetry chapbook, *Poppy Seeds*, which has been released as a spoken word album on Spotify. Her full length collection of poems, *Spread Thick*, was published by Finishing Line Press in September 2022. Her work has been published online, in print, and was featured in a solo show at the Lanecia Rouse Tinsley Gallery in 2022. Sara, her partner Mitch, and their three children spent half of 2022 traveling through 34 states and then settled in Nacogdoches, Texas to be near family and give gardening a shot again. Links to other work can be found at saratrianamitchell.com.

- ❖ **Sarah Lofgren** is a copywriter living in Seattle who creates odd speculative fiction in her free time. She also enjoys digital illustration and choreographing modern dances. For more info, visit sarahlofgren.com.

- ❖ **Shan Cawley** (she/her/hers) is an Appalachian writer and PhD student hailing from West Virginia. You can follow Shan on Instagram @dr.idiot_

- ❖ **Sherry Shahan** (she/her) is a teal-haired septuagenarian who writes in a small beach town. Her poetry lives in national and international literary journals and anthologies. She holds an MFA from Vermont College of Fine Arts and has been nominated for The Pushcart Prize in Poetry (2024) and The Pushcart Prize in Short Fiction (2025).

- ❖ **Vignette-Noelle Lammott** (she/her) is a disciple of beauty, heavily inspired by the Transcendentalists. Poet, photographer and scholar of antiquarian works, she lives a quiet life in southern New Jersey.

- ❖ **Violet Piper** (she/her) is a Brooklyn-based writer and journalist.

- ❖ **Wilfred Jensen** (They/Them) is a queer-trans poet and international student from Denmark who recently graduated from Indiana State University. Their work has appeared in Indiana State University's student creative writing and visual arts journal, *Allusions*, and they were a recipient of the National Society of Arts and Letters, Indiana Chapter, Helen and Lynton Caldwell Memorial Award 2022 and the Engber Merit Award 2023. They love their cat and obsessively write letters to their found family.

- ❖ **Xavier Zane Wherley** (they/them) is an author and poet with a BA in Creative Writing from Capital University. Being genderqueer, homosexual, and on the Autism Spectrum, they share with us an atypical viewpoint and hope to broaden your perspective.

- ❖ **Zephyris** has enjoyed more than two decades as a writing instructor, where they've sculpted minds, and kindled the flames of creativity and fervor. Zephyris is gender queer, and advocates fiercely for their own two children who are gay and trans.